THE
ONE O'CLOCK
CHOP

THE
ONE O'CLOCK
CHOP

Ralph Fletcher

Henry Holt and Company • New York

I am grateful to Janice Furuta, Liana Honda, Jody Kawamata-Chang,
Ronnie Kopp, Anna Lum Lee, Miki Maeshiro, Merle Matsuda, Nani
Pai, and JoAnn Wong-Kam. They provided invaluable perspectives
about being a teenage girl in Hawaii during the 1970s. In writing
this book I also drew on recollections from Joseph Fletcher,
Elaine Fletcher, and Betsy Mooney about what it was like
to be a teenager on Long Island, New York, in 1973.

Henry Holt and Company, LLC
Publishers since 1866
175 Fifth Avenue
New York, New York 10010
www.HenryHoltKids.com

Henry Holt® is a registered trademark of Henry Holt and Company, LLC.
Copyright © 2007 by Ralph Fletcher
All rights reserved.
Distributed in Canada by H. B. Fenn and Company Ltd.

Library of Congress Cataloging-in-Publication Data
The one o'clock chop / Ralph Fletcher.—1st ed.
p.   cm.
Summary: In New York, fourteen-year-old Matt spends the summer of
1973 digging clams to earn money for his own boat and falling for Jazzy, a
beautiful and talented girl from Hawaii who happens to be his first cousin.
ISBN-13: 978-0-8050-8143-5 / ISBN-10: 0-8050-8143-7
[1. Clamming—Fiction. 2. Boats and boating—Fiction. 3. Cousins—Fiction.
4. Single-parent families—Fiction. 5. New York (N.Y.)—Fiction.
6. New York (State)—History—20th century—Fiction.] I. Title.
PZ7.F632115On 2007   [Fic]—dc22   2006035470

First edition—2007 / Designed by Meredith Pratt
Printed in the United States of America on acid-free paper. ∞

1   3   5   7   9   10   8   6   4   2

For my sister Elaine,
who remembers that year
and tells the best stories

THE
ONE O'CLOCK
CHOP

jAZZY

SUMMER OF 1973. The newspaper headlines were all about the Watergate scandal. The Vietnam War had officially ended in January, but American planes were still dropping bombs nearby in Laos and Cambodia. There was lots of baseball news, too. Nolan Ryan pitched his second no-hitter; Hank Aaron hit home run number 700.

But it was Jasmine McKenzie who made the biggest headline in my life, a girl who happened to be my first cousin. I never dreamed that I'd fall in love with her when she visited us from Hawaii, but that's what happened.

Jazzy loved all kinds of music: folk, pop, rock, traditional Hawaiian, big band, and jazz, too. She explained to me how jazz is different from other music. Many jazz musicians don't play music that's been written down ahead of time. In jazz there's something called improvisation, where the musicians decide what to play right then, spontaneous, unplanned. They bounce off notes the other musicians play. They follow the spirit of the music, letting it carry them to a new place every time. They make it up as they go along.

I guess that's what Jazzy and I were doing that summer. We were in brand-new territory, at least I was. I couldn't fall back on what I knew about girls. With Jazzy I had to make it up as we went along.

DAN PIERSALL

"'Wise man,' four letters."

Mom glanced over at me; I didn't have any idea.

"'Sage.'" She wrote it down.

We were sitting side by side at the kitchen table. There was a fat wedge of morning sun warming my shoulders. I yawned, feeling too lazy to focus on the crossword puzzle. Doing the crossword felt a little too much like school, which I wanted to forget, since my summer vacation had just started. I had to make myself pay attention. Mom and I did the crossword every weekend morning, and most other days. It was our tradition.

"'Sea eagle,' three letters," she said. "'Ern,' that fits."

Mom was a crossword whiz. When she got on a roll she was unstoppable. IOU: chit. Lunar New Year: tet. Semimonthly tide: neap. Slow down: notsofast. The crossword puzzle was like another language, and Mom could speak it better than anyone I knew.

"How do you *know* all this stuff?"

"You pick it up along the way." Mom smiled. "'A.L. pitcher Ryan.'"

"'Nolan,'" I said. That was my main contribution, helping out with sports clues, though I suspected she probably knew most of them, too.

"'Don Ho song,' eleven letters," Mom said. "'Tiny Bubbles.'"

"Who is Don Ho?"

"A Hawaiian singer," she replied. "Which reminds me. Your cousin Jazzy is coming in less than a week. She's spending the summer with us."

"I know, you told me." The whole summer. It seemed like a long time. I wasn't sure how I felt about it.

"Do you remember her?"

"Sort of." She was almost a year older than me. I had dim memories of playing with her in a pool when we were little. And I knew the basic story. Years ago, Mom's oldest brother, Neal, was stationed in Oahu, Hawaii, with the U.S. Air Force. He fell in love with Yvonne, a native Hawaiian, and they had a baby. When Jazzy was four, Neal was killed in a motorcycle accident. Now my cousin lived near Honolulu.

Her mom had to go to the Philippines to take care of Jazzy's grandmother, who'd gotten sick, so Mom invited Jazzy to spend the summer with us. She had always wanted to see New York.

"I don't have to entertain her all the time, do I?" I asked.

"Of course not." Mom stood up to pour herself more coffee. "Her mother said she's quite independent."

"I've got plans this summer," I told her. "I'm trying to buy my boat."

I had my eyes on a Boston Whaler. A used Whaler, with a good thirty-five- or forty-horsepower engine, would run about nine hundred dollars, which was nine hundred dollars more than I had.

"Technically, you can't say 'my boat' until you buy it," she teased. "How do you plan on getting the money? Have you thought of asking your father?"

"No!" I said, louder than I meant. My parents divorced about four years ago. My father lived in Whitefish, Montana. He had a new wife, and he had money—I knew if I mentioned the Boston Whaler he'd probably buy it for me. But I wanted to pay for it with my own money.

"Why not?" Mom asked.

"Because. Just promise you won't mention it to him."

"Okay, I promise." She looked at me. "How's the job search going?"

"Not great." I had tried all the usual suspects—McDonald's, Dunkin' Donuts, and the local hardware store, plus a greasy spoon called the Golden Egg that was famous for outrageous omelets—but I struck out. I tried the concession stands at Fire Island beaches, but they weren't hiring, either. Nobody had any openings.

"I know someone," Mom said casually. "A professional clam digger. It's possible he might let you work with him."

"Digging clams?" I gave her my most skeptical look.

"His name is Dan Piersall, and he owes me a favor."

"A favor?"

"I took care of his mother when I was doing home care a few years ago," she said. "I'll give him a call."

"Okay."

"C'mon, help me finish this puzzle. We're almost done. 'Basketball target.'"

"'Hoop'?" I suggested.

"No, three letters." She pursed her lips. "'Net' doesn't fit."

"'Rim,'" I said.

She grinned. "You're a genius."

▪   ▪   ▪

That afternoon I biked over to Dan Piersall's house and rang the doorbell. The man who answered the door had a red, weathered face. I figured he was around Mom's age, maybe older, though he was built like a weight lifter. Huge pecs. Gorilla arms. His hand practically swallowed mine when we shook. He motioned me to follow him inside. The kitchen was a no-frills, bare-bones kind of place. Nothing on the walls. A mixed bacon-and-coffee smell hung in the air.

"Your mother says you're looking for a job." He held up the coffeepot.

"No," I said (to the coffee). "Yes" (to the job).

"You want to dig clams?"

"I guess so."

"Clamming can be brutal work, but the money's decent." When Dan lifted the coffee cup, his biceps stretched the sleeve of his T-shirt. This guy was really jacked. "You could clear a hundred, maybe even a hundred fifty, bucks a week after you get the hang of it. If you're willing to work. And you get paid, cash, every day."

I pictured a wad of tens and twenties in my wallet. At a hundred fifty dollars a week, I could easily buy the Boston Whaler by the end of the summer.

"There are some start-up costs," Dan said. "Most of the professional clammers are tongers, like me. Clam tongs run around a hundred fifty bucks, but I've got an extra set you can use for now. You're going to have to buy a clamming license. You can get one at the town hall on Monday morning."

"How much is that?" I asked.

"A one-week clamming license goes for twenty bucks."

I nodded, trying to wrap my brain around the idea. Me: Clam Digger. It was far different from any other summer job I'd applied for.

"I don't know anything about digging clams," I admitted.

"You'll learn." Dan crossed his thick arms. "OJT."

"Huh?"

"On-the-job training. It's not hard to learn. I can show you the basics. But I want to make one thing clear. I'm not guaranteeing you a job. A couple years ago I let another guy work with me and it was a disaster. I don't want to go through that again. I'll give you a tryout, one week, to see if clamming suits you. Okay?"

"Okay."

"Meet me at the dock Tuesday morning at seven o'clock sharp." Dan finished the last of his coffee. "My boat's a

Garvey, the *Morrison Hotel*. Wear some old clothes. Bring lunch. And lots of water."

It sounded simple. Clams, money, Boston Whaler. Those words had a nice sound, smooth and mellow. The last thing I pictured that night before I fell asleep were Dan's bulging biceps, and I was thinking muscles like that would look mighty fine on me.

LiTTLEnECKS AnD CHERRYSTOnES

I WOKE UP AT SIX, but I spaced out in the shower, and by the time I dried off it was already six fourteen. I threw on some clothes, flew downstairs, made a sloppy peanut butter and jelly sandwich, grabbed a thermos of water, and raced out of the house still licking jelly from my fingers. I didn't want to be late on the first day.

It only took ten minutes to ride my bike to the dock. I locked it to the chain-link fence and found the *Morrison Hotel* moored at the far end. It was a Garvey with a flat deck. It had a small cabin in back with windows on three sides. Nothing fancy. A VIETNAM VETERAN sticker hung on one window. Dan stood at the bow wearing a T-shirt, old jeans, and tall rubber boots. I suddenly felt underdressed in a pair of ripped shorts and old sneakers. He looked me up and down.

"You got your license?" he asked.

"Yeah." Yesterday Mom drove me to the town hall and wrote out a check for twenty dollars. I promised to pay her back.

"Good, I don't want those Conservation officers making a courtesy visit to my boat. Let's go, untie those lines. We're two minutes late."

The *Morrison Hotel* was powered by a 125-horsepower outboard Evinrude mounted on the stern. With one short pull, Dan started the engine. He put it into reverse and eased the boat away from the dock. I stood next to the cabin as we slipped down the still waters of the canal, dead slow, with the sun low on the horizon. On both sides of the canal I could see lush lawns being fed by expensive sprinkler systems, the big houses filled with rich kids sound asleep at this early hour.

Suddenly I heard music. Loud.

"The Doors." Dan motioned for me to sit next to him. "I always play the Doors to start the day. Gets my blood moving. This record is *Morrison Hotel*—I named my boat after it."

I sat next to Dan, but the engine fumes started making me sick to my stomach, so I went to the bow and sat cross-legged on the deck. Another clam boat motored up from behind and moved alongside us. The driver had a tanned face and a huge gut.

"Got a new mascot, huh?" he yelled to Dan, motioning at me.

"We'll see," Dan replied with a short wave.

When we reached the mouth of the bay, Dan pushed the throttle forward, and the boat picked up speed. He pushed the volume on the music up too. The cool air felt great against my face. Straight ahead I could see the bridge for the Robert Moses Causeway that led to Captree Island. Already the bridge traffic was heavy with tourists heading over to the beaches. We drove another fifteen minutes before Dan cut the engine and killed the music. Total quiet.

"Get your bearings," Dan said, moving to the front of the boat. "This is the Great South Bay. Land is back there, to the north. Fire Island is over there, dead south. If you go west you'll hit New York City. The Hamptons and Montauk are northeast."

I nodded. I've always had a good sense of direction.

"It's your job to drop anchor."

I started to pick it up but Dan grabbed my arm. "Wait 'til we're done drifting. . . . Okay, throw it in. Feed out the line, and let the wind ease us back 'til it's set. Feel it?"

I held on to the line until I felt the anchor dig into the bottom. "How deep is it here?"

"Only eight feet," he said. "C'mon, grab your tongs."

Clam tongs are a weird-looking contraption—oversized scissors with twelve-foot wooden handles connected to a set of metal teeth at the end.

"Watch," Dan said. "You hold the tong handles and let them slide down 'til you feel the teeth hit bottom. Okay? You work the handles together to close the basket."

Muscles jumping, Dan pulled the handles until they came together. "What do I do now?"

I shrugged. "See what you got?"

"Thing is, what I've got now is a bunch of bay muck, and it weighs a ton. First I've gotta shake out the mud." He raised the tongs about one foot and shook them up and down. I heard something rattling under the water. Dan lifted the tongs in one smooth motion and spilled six clams onto the deck. There was a bunch of seaweed and other stuff, too. Dan picked up a clam and showed it to me.

"Littleneck clams. These bigger ones are cherrystones. This is the reason we bust our butts out here. These tasty little critters are served in the finest restaurants all over the world. Go on, kid, give it a try."

I lowered the tongs until I could feel them hit bottom, and started working the handles together, letting the teeth slide through the muck at the bottom of the bay. It felt kind of creepy, and I tried not to imagine what was down there.

I worked the tongs shut, lifted them to shake out the mud, and pulled them up hand over hand. It was easy until the heavy head came out of the water and I had to lift the tongs onto the deck. When I opened the teeth, four clams clattered out. I couldn't help smiling.

"There you go." Dan nodded. "A bushel of littlenecks is going for forty bucks right now."

"How many clams to a bushel?" I asked.

"Five hundred and fifty, depending on the size of the clams, or seventy pounds," he said. "You're almost one percent of the way there. Start at the bow and work back to the stern. Happy clamming."

I grabbed my set of tongs and moved to the front of the boat. This is going to be a cinch, I told myself. I could already picture my Boston Whaler skimming across the Great South Bay.

THE ONE O'CLOCK CHOP

WHAT A JOB! I would get to work outside all day in the fresh air and sunshine. Standing on the deck, working my tongs shut, I felt the muscles burn in my chest and arms. If nothing else, this summer job was definitely going to get me tanned and ripped.

Tongs down, push the handles together, rinse off the mud, haul it up, and see what I got. Dan kept playing music by the Doors, but the sound of the clams rattling onto the deck was music enough for me. It sounded like money.

But I soon realized it was going to be harder than it looked. A lot harder. Imagine lifting weights, the same two exercises, squeeze and lift, squeeze and lift, hour after hour, with the sun beating down.

By eight fifteen I had broken a sweat.

By nine I was gulping water.

By ten the cabin thermometer read 81 degrees.

By ten thirty my stomach was growling. I scarfed down my PB and J sandwich.

I could hear the continuous clatter on Dan's side of the boat as he pulled up eight, ten clams at a time. It seemed like my tiny pile of clams hardly grew at all. I pulled up two, then one, none, none. I let out a grunt of frustration.

"Hit a dry spot?" Dan asked. "Move back up to where you were getting them before."

I tried that and it worked. Four. Five. Four.

By eleven thirty my arms felt like rubber and there was a funny taste in my mouth. I gulped some water but I was about to pass out, I was so hungry.

"Stop for lunch?" Dan asked.

I mumbled an okay. Truth was, I'd already eaten everything I brought on board. Dan ducked into the cabin.

"Here." He handed me a sandwich, a bag of chips, and three oversized cookies.

"But what about—?"

"Don't worry, I'm not giving you my lunch," he said. "I brought extra today. Tomorrow you'll pack more food."

"Thanks." Embarrassed, I went forward and found a shady spot by the cabin. The tuna sandwich was thick, with slices of onion and Swiss cheese. Nothing had ever tasted so good.

Suddenly, there was a flutter of wings. A big seagull landed on the bow not five feet from me!

"Whoa!" I jumped and almost knocked my food overboard.

"Meet the famous Bert," Dan said. Smiling, he tossed the seagull a broken clam; the bird caught it neatly in his beak. "He stops by every day around this time. I'm his meal ticket. Bert and I go way back. He knows all my secrets, but he never tells a soul."

Dan sat on the deck and leaned back against the cabin. I wondered what secrets a guy like Dan might have. While we ate, Bert picked the meat from broken clams on the deck. I spotted a cluster of clam boats in the distance.

"How come those clammers are all bunched together like that?"

"Because most people are sheep—they just follow everyone else, without thinking. Most of those guys are just posers. They don't really work. They just fart around, chewing the fat, drinking beer." Dan spat into the water. "I mean, why come out here if you don't want to work?"

He passed me a plum, cold and juicy.

"You're getting red, kid. I'd put on more sunscreen, if I was you." Dan stood and stretched. "Okay, back to work. We quit at four. That's three more hours, and I'm going to make them count."

I picked up my set of tongs. The bay had been like one large sheet of polished glass, but now I detected a sudden breeze from the south. You could actually see it coming toward us from Fire Island, roughening up the smooth surface.

"That's the One O'Clock Chop," Dan explained. "The old salts say you can set your watch by it."

When the breeze reached us, our boat swung around on its anchor until it faced south. The other boats followed suit. The breeze was gentle at first, but it got stronger as the afternoon went on, rocking the boat, making it harder to set the tongs and keep them in one place.

"Whoooo!" I looked up to see two girls in bathing suits sailing past on a Sunfish, their dark hair streaming in the wind. I recognized one of the girls—Darlene LeClerc. She'd been in my algebra class last year; I remembered that she was on the gymnastics team. Darlene waved happily; I waved back. The Sunfish flew across the water, whipped by the stiff southern breeze. The girls were laughing, without a care in the world. I felt jealous watching them, wishing I could be out there laughing and skimming over the surface of the bay instead of here trying to haul up clams from the mucky bottom.

At three forty-five I sat down on the deck, exhausted. I could barely lift my arms, let alone the tongs. My bushel basket was full, though.

"How'd you do?" Dan asked.

"A bushel," I said proudly.

"Let's take a look." He took out a shallow box that had four metal bars on the bottom, evenly spaced. "First we gotta run 'em through the cull rack. Dump some in here."

I hoisted the bushel basket and spilled about two dozen clams into the cull rack. It made a loud noise when Dan shook it, and five clams fell through the iron bars and onto the deck.

"Those are seed, baby clams," Dan explained, kicking them overboard. "They're tasty as hell, melt in your mouth. But you gotta throw them back unless you're eager to pay a thousand-dollar fine to Conservation."

Dan dumped the good clams into an empty bushel basket. When we finished culling them, the wire basket was about three-quarters full. I let out a groan of disappointment.

"Hey, that's not too bad for your first day," he told me. Then he went to work on his pile of clams. Dan ended up with three bushels even. He counted out fifty clams and put them in a separate bag. We dumped all the clams into brown burlap sacks. When I got my clamming license, the guy at the Conservation Department gave me a box of tags, each with my license number printed on it. That way they could track down any clammer who sold bad clams. I attached one of my tags to the burlap bag containing the clams I'd dug. Dan did the same with his three sacks. Then he went to the back of the boat and restarted the engine.

"Pull the anchor," he yelled. He handed me a push broom and plastic bucket. "Clean the mud and junk off the deck. I'll drive slow."

He cranked the Doors and we headed in.

When we got to the fishing dock, Dan turned down the music. Three big trucks were backed up to the dock. As the boat eased into a slip, I jumped onto the dock and tied off the line. Dan killed the engine. A bushel of clams weighs seventy pounds, but Dan lifted them up to me like they were light as pillows. Carrying a bushel in each hand, he brought them to the truck parked in the middle of the other two. I followed with my sack of clams. On the side of the truck I read the words

FRANK DIFEO
CLAM WHOLESALER

"Daniel," the man said, grinning. He wore a white shirt and had a thick gold chain around his neck.

"Hello, Frank. This is Matt. He's gonna be working with me this summer."

"A rookie, huh?" Frank smiled and took my clams. "Let's see what you got, kid."

There was a scale on the truck. Frank put my burlap bag on it. From my angle it looked like the needle hit the mark right at fifty-five pounds.

"Fifty-four," Frank said. "Damn good for a first day."

He peeled off three ten-dollar bills, gave them to me, and shook my hand. Dan's clams came to two hundred and ten pounds. Frank handed him six crisp twenties.

"See you guys tomorrow!" Frank said.

"C'mon." Dan was holding the small bag of clams. "I'll give you a ride home."

"Thanks." I was so tired I could barely talk. With one hand Dan lifted my bike onto the back of his truck. I climbed into the front seat. When we got to my house, Dan picked up the small sack and followed me inside.

"Well, hello there." Mom smiled. "It's nice to see you, Dan."

"Hello, Alice."

Mom studied me closely. "He looks pretty roasted, doesn't he?"

"Well done," Dan agreed. He handed her the burlap sack. "I brought you some clams. You can't get them any fresher than that."

"What a treat, Dan! Would you like to stay and have supper with us?"

"Thanks. Maybe another time." Dan looked at me. "Seven a.m., Matt. Don't forget your clam license. We've got a busy week ahead."

"On the Fourth of July?" Mom asked. "That's a holiday."

"I'll be clamming." Dan eyed me. "It's up to you, kid."

I nodded. "I'll be there."

After Dan left, Mom looked me up and down. "You must be beat! Would you like a glass of lemonade? I just made some. Oh, you got a letter from your father."

"Okay." I sounded like some kind of zombie. I wandered into the den and collapsed on the couch. There was nothing on TV but trashy sitcoms, which suited me fine. All I wanted was to sit in a cool place where I wouldn't have to move a muscle.

After a while I went to my room and opened the letter from Dad.

Dear Matt,

Howdy! How is your job search going? I want to hear all about it. Let me know if I can help. And hey, what's with those Mets? They can't hit worth a lick, but they're in first place. Go figure. Anyway, I miss you, kid. Talk to you Friday.

Love,

Dad

I tried to remember how it was when Dad lived with us. Those memories were fading. When he and Mom split, he moved out west and immediately fell in love with Heather, who was ten years younger than Mom and real pretty. Now he was selling life insurance and building a new house in the mountains, so I guessed business was good.

I started getting that pissed-off feeling. The way he just left, moved away, and got remarried, bing, bang, boom. Dad and Mom fought pretty much nonstop the last year they were together, so maybe their marriage wasn't meant to last. But why did he have to move two thousand miles away from me? He couldn't sell life insurance around here? I missed him a lot. I didn't see him very often, but he phoned every Friday afternoon at four o'clock, and I never missed that call.

I took out a notebook and carefully wrote down the date, weight of the clams I'd dug, and how much money I'd earned. Then I stripped off my clothes and staggered into the bathroom. The shower felt great on my back and neck.

For supper Mom cooked the clams Dan brought, serving them with melted butter. Usually I could devour steamed clams by the dozen, but tonight I couldn't even look at them. After supper I went straight to my room and flopped on my bed. The phone rang. It was Trevor, my best friend.

"Hello, Squire." For some reason he'd been calling me that since sixth grade. "Want to come over and hang out for a while?"

"Nah, I'm beat," I told him. "I can't."

When I hung up the phone and closed my eyes, all I could see were billions and billions of clams.

July 4

STEALING HOME

WHEN THE ALARM SOUNDED AT SIX I was still dressed in my shirt and jeans. And I felt awful: sore neck, sore arms, sore everything. My shoulders burned. More than anything I wanted to roll over, close my eyes, and sink into unconsciousness. But then a picture of that Boston Whaler swam into my mind, and I wrenched myself out of bed.

"Morning, Matt." Mom was sitting at the kitchen table, reading the paper. I noticed the headlines.

NIXON PLANS TO SPEAK OUT
ON WATERGATE AFTER END
OF THE CURRENT HEARINGS

"You pooped out at seven o'clock last night!"

"I was wiped out."

"I made you two sandwiches for lunch."

"Better make it three," I told her. "Okay, Mom?"

"You got it."

I poured myself a bowl of Cheerios and watched Mom wrestling with a new jar of jelly, trying to open it. She worked as a nurse at the hospital's cardiac unit, and when her arthritis got bad it was hard for her to stand on her feet all day.

But Mom's no wimp. She's an expert at "making a stink," and getting in somebody's face when she has to. In third grade my teacher, Mrs. Occhiogrosso, made my life miserable. For some reason this lady really had it in for me. When Mom saw my report card she went ballistic, marched down to the principal, and told him, "I send a boy to school who is well-loved, well-fed, healthy, and curious, and his teacher sends him home saying he's a failure. Well, I want to know who's the failure?" She insisted that the principal move me out of Mrs. Occhiogrosso's class and refused to budge from his office until he finally agreed.

"I've got a busy day at the hospital," Mom was saying. "And I want to get the guest room fixed up nice for your cousin. I might stop and pick up some curtains on the way home from work. Don't you think that would look nice?"

"Sure, whatever."

I was half looking forward to Jazzy's visit and half dreading it. What would she be like? What if she turned out to be boring or spoiled? Besides, I wasn't absolutely sure I wanted someone living with us. After Dad moved out, things were bumpy at home at first. But now Mom and I knew how to work together.

I grabbed my lunch. "Gotta go."

"Wait," she said. "You'd better let me put some lotion on your shoulders and neck."

The morning began same as the day before, only this time Dan didn't need to tell me what to do. While he started the engine, I untied the bowline and held the boat away from the dock as he backed out of the slip. Then he turned on the first Doors song of the day—"Light My Fire"—and we headed out to the bay. A half hour later he cut the engine and I set the anchor.

I winced when Dan passed me my set of tongs. There was a nasty blister on the palm of one hand, and the water made it sting. Dan and I worked on opposite sides of the boat again. I pulled up clams, plus a lot of other weird stuff—crabs, skinny scungilli shells, seaweed, rocks, and a yellow sponge that kept getting caught on the teeth of the tongs. I wore a T-shirt and baseball cap. There wasn't a cloud in the sky to block the sun, and I didn't want my sunburn to get any worse. I could feel my arms, chest, neck, and back all screaming, NOT THIS AGAIN!

A wave of nausea rolled over me. I put down the tongs and leaned back against the cabin.

"You okay?" Dan asked.

I didn't answer. Dan walked over to me.

"Sit down. Put your head between your legs. Take some deep breaths. You eat breakfast?"

I nodded and sat down. The rocking of the boat was making me dizzy. I stuck my head over the side and hung there two feet above the water. Cold sweat snaked down my back. I tried to throw up, but I couldn't. Finally, I sat up.

"Take it slow." Dan handed me my water. "Don't rush it."

"I think I'm okay." After another few minutes, I grabbed the tongs and went back to work. My body started doing what it was supposed to do. I was feeling, well, not especially good, but like I might be able to get through the day after all.

At noon we took our lunch break. This time, thanks to Mom, I actually had enough food of my own to eat. Bert made his feathery entrance a few minutes later. The seagull looked annoyed that we didn't have a bunch of cracked clams arranged and waiting for him.

"What do you think this is?" Dan asked Bert, laughing. "Some kinda restaurant?"

"How long have you been clamming?" I asked Dan.

"Twenty-one years." He took a bite of his sandwich.

"Do you like it?"

"It pays the bills." He shrugged. "Unless you got a father named Rockefeller, most of us have to work."

"You told me to buy the one-week license," I said. "Why didn't you tell me to buy the one-year license?"

"I wasn't sure you'd last more than a week."

"What do you think now?" I asked.

"The jury's still out." Dan looked at me. "You ask a lot of questions, kid. You want to talk about politics? Tricky Dick Nixon? Watergate? Vietnam?"

I didn't know what to say to that. Dan tossed a piece of crust to Bert; the seagull caught it neatly in the air.

"Bert and I don't do much chitchatting," Dan said. "But over the years we've come to understand each other."

I translated that to mean "shut up." Which is what I did.

Dan stayed quiet in the afternoon, and I was glad when he turned on the radio so we could listen to the Mets game. The sound of the crowd got me thinking about my father. He was a huge baseball fan, and he made me one, too. Because of him, I knew tons of baseball trivia. I knew that Willie Mays hit his first home run off pitcher Warren Spahn. And I knew that Tony Cloninger, a pitcher, once hit two grand slams in the same game. Dad took me to Yankee Stadium or

Shea Stadium a couple of times a year, and I can remember those games like they happened yesterday—the lights, the smell of popcorn and beer, how amazingly green the field looked when you walked up from the concourse into the stadium.

"Maybe the batter will steal first base," I said one time when I was about four or five.

Dad laughed. "You can't steal first base."

"Can you steal second base?" I asked.

"Sure. If you get on first you can steal second or third. You can even steal home!"

"Really?"

"You bet. Maury Wills stole home a couple of times. Jackie Robinson was good at stealing home, too. That's one of the most exciting plays in baseball."

Stealing home. That idea fascinated me. Later, after my parents' divorce, I kept hoping my father might "steal home," might sneak back into our house late one night. I'd wake up to find him the next morning sprawled in the big bed, and things would be like before. I hung on to that hope for a long time, until I realized that it wasn't ever going to happen.

Finally, it was four o'clock. After we culled our clams, I finished with three-quarters of a bushel, just what I'd dug the day before. Dan had dug three bushels and a peck, which is a quarter of a bushel. When we headed in to the dock, I noticed wholesalers and other clammers checking out the mound of clams on our boat. I felt proud having my clams sacked next to Dan's.

According to Frank's scales, I dug fifty-six pounds of clams. He paid me thirty-one dollars, which, by my calculations, was a dollar less than he should have paid me. But I didn't care. Minimum wage was $1.60 an hour—at that rate I would have earned less than thirteen dollars today. I was so tired I could hardly stuff my wallet back into my jeans.

Over the next couple of days, my life followed the same routine. Eight hours of clamming in the sun felt like getting busted over the head with a two-by-four. I'd drag myself home, tired and blistered raw, shower, eat dinner, and fall into bed by nine thirty. I had no energy to do anything else. Fun-wise, it was pathetic. But the shoe box under my bed was steadily filling up with tens and twenties.

"So what do you think about clamming?" Dan asked at the end of my first week on the job. "Boring?"

"Kind of . . . monotonous," I admitted. "Not that I'm complaining."

"I've never found this job boring. Life is about change, that's what the Buddhists say. Every day out here I notice changes, little and big. One afternoon the water's a shade of green blue I've never seen before. Or maybe I see a sun dog at the horizon. Or get a whiff of bacon blown from the shore. Each day is a bit different. Hey, your clamming license expires on Monday."

"Yeah."

"Are you going to renew it?"

I shrugged uncertainly. "Can I?"

Dan nodded and tossed a peach pit overboard. "Sure. You're a keeper."

So that afternoon I went back to the town hall and laid down five twenty-dollar bills for a one-year clamming license.

The following Friday, I spotted Trevor as we were heading back to the Babylon docks. He was leaning against the fence by the parking lot. After I sold my clams, I walked over.

"Yo, Squire." Trevor smacked my right arm, hard.

"Don't," I said, wincing.

"I thought you were a big-time clamming moose." He laughed. "You know, it's Friday the thirteenth. You feeling unlucky?"

At that moment a girl appeared, walking down the grassy hill that led from the parking lot to the dock. Tanned. Long black hair. A white blouse with white shorts. Trevor and I stood watching her come toward us. She had a nice, easy kind of walk, not look-how-cool-I-am, but not shy, either. There was a white flower in her hair, just above her ear. Mom followed a step behind her.

"This is Jazzy." Mom smiled. "Jazzy, meet Matt."

The afternoon was already sunny, but when Jazzy smiled it felt like someone switched on a high-watt lamp.

"Hi," I said. For one panicky second I wondered if I was supposed to hug or kiss her. Jazzy reached out to shake my hand.

"I'm all dirty," I warned.

"Yeah, he stinks," Trevor agreed. "It's a new perfume: Essence de Clam."

Laughing, Jazzy squeezed my grimy hand in hers.

"Matt, why don't you introduce your friend?" Mom suggested.

"This is Trevor," I said. "He's going to summer school because he flunked geometry."

"And this is dork Matt," Trevor put in.

"Doormat?" Jazzy giggled.

"Exactly." Trevor nodded. "But don't worry. He's harmless."

"I brought you something," Jazzy said. She placed a necklace around my neck and kissed me on the cheek. A sweet smell flooded my nostrils—the necklace was made from fresh flowers. I felt as silly and gaudy as a peacock standing on the docks, filthy with clam gore and tropical flowers around my neck. I wanted to take off the necklace, but Mom gave me a look, and I kept it on.

"A flower lei." Mom leaned forward to smell the flowers. "That's the traditional Hawaiian greeting. Isn't it lovely? You should see the one she gave me at the airport."

Now Jazzy stepped back to take my picture.

"Don't—" I began, but she snapped a picture anyway.

"Do you two remember each other?" Mom asked.

"I remember we were in one of those plastic kiddie pools," Jazzy said. "You squirted me with a hose."

"He still does that!" Trevor chimed in.

I elbowed Trevor as we all started moving from the dock toward the parking lot. In the photographs I'd seen of Jazzy, she was a little kid. But she sure looked different now.

SETTLING IN

AFTER DINNER, Jazzy handed out the presents she had brought: Kona coffee, chocolate-covered macadamia nuts, a puka-shell necklace for Mom. She slipped over my head something that looked like a green rope.

"You already gave me one," I protested.

"This is a special lei for men," Jazzy explained. "It's made out of tea leaves. I brought some pictures, too."

Jazzy took out a small photo album. The first picture showed her standing beside a woman.

"That's my mom," Jazzy said. "She's the best. Right now she's helping my grandma."

"I hope Grandma is going to be all right," Mom murmured.

Next we looked at a picture of a little girl sitting on a man's lap. They were both grinning. The man wore a sweatshirt with the words BIRD IS THE WORD in big letters.

"That's my brother," Mom said softly.

"That picture was taken right before my dad died in the motorcycle accident," Jazzy explained. "I was about four."

Eyes shining, Mom looked at Jazzy. "He was crazy about you. Do you remember much about him?"

Jazzy nodded solemnly. "He loved music. And he told some great stories."

"What's up with the sweatshirt?" I asked.

"Bird was Charlie Parker's nickname," Jazzy explained.

I gave her a blank look.

"You never heard of Charlie Parker?" Jazzy looked shocked. "He was only the greatest jazz saxophone player in history. He played with Dizzy Gillespie. Jazz was my dad's favorite music."

The phone rang.

"Hello?" I said.

"Is this Matt?" a woman asked.

"Yes." I recognized the voice as Mrs. Jacobsen, my father's secretary.

"Please hold for a call from your father," she said.

I looked at Mom. "I'll pick up in the den."

This was how Dad's weekly telephone call always began. His secretary called and got me on the line. Then I had to wait, sometimes for a whole minute or two, until my father came on. I knew he was busy, but it annoyed me that he didn't pick up the phone and dial my number himself.

"Matt!" he cried. "How are you?"

"Good. My cousin Jazzy's visiting us. She's staying for the summer."

"Jazzy? The little girl from Hawaii?"

"Uh-huh." I didn't bother mentioning that the "little girl" was now fifteen years old.

"Well, that's terrific, give her my best. So how's the clamming going? That's got to be tough physical labor."

"It's hard, but I'm getting the hang of it. I made a hundred and twenty-five dollars last week."

"Way to go! Hard work never hurt anybody. How's the weather out there, Matt? It's been in the high nineties here in Montana."

He told me about a wildfire that was raging less than twenty miles away. Next he began updating me on the construction of his new house. He was having trouble getting workers to show up on time.

"Nobody wants to work anymore!" he exclaimed. "Wait a sec, I need to put you on hold. I'll be right back."

For the next sixty seconds I sat holding the phone, feeling slightly stupid.

"I'm sorry, Matt, I'd better get going," Dad said when he

finally came back on the line. "Things are berserk around here today. I'll call you next week, okay?"

"Okay. Bye, Dad."

That night Jazzy felt jet-lagged, so she went to bed at nine o'clock. I crashed soon after.

The next day was Saturday, so I didn't get out of bed until ten. Mom made a huge breakfast: omelets with home fries—real oniony, the way I love them—buttery rolls, bacon *and* sausage, plus a fruit salad. Jazzy had an appetite to match mine.

"This tastes so good, Aunt Alice!" Jazzy smiled.

"Enjoy." Mom sipped her coffee, watching us eat. "Matt, more bacon? Another roll?"

"Sure, Mom."

"What kinds of things would you like to do while you're in New York?" Mom asked Jazzy.

"Don't worry about me," Jazzy said. "I'll be happy with whatever you plan. Seriously."

Mom smiled. "Well, I'm glad to hear that. But I want you to have a good time. You came all the way from Hawaii! We could take the train into Manhattan and do some shopping. There's a place where you can get half-price Broadway tickets. Would you like to see a play?"

"I'd *love* to see a play!" Jazzy said eagerly. "And I'm dying to go to Greenwich Village."

The doorbell rang. It was Trevor. He had a beach towel wrapped, turbanlike, around his head.

"Hot, hot." He jumped up and down on the porch like some kind of demented orangutan. "Water. Swim. Ahhh."

I glared at him. After working all week under the beating sun, the idea of lying on a beach didn't exactly thrill me. My idea of fun would be to hole up in a dark movie theater with a tub of popcorn and a few Cokes.

Jazzy came to the door; she smiled when she recognized Trevor. "Hello. Are we going swimming?"

I could feel her eyes on me, waiting.

"I'm already sunburned," I protested.

"C'mon, let's go to the beach!" Jazzy begged.

"Oh, all right," I reluctantly agreed.

It was a fifteen-minute walk to Wheelright Pond. A plane droned overhead, pulling a sign that said COUNTY FAIR OPENS SATURDAY NIGHT AT 7 P.M.

"Tonight's the first night of the fair," Trevor pointed out.

"That's fair-ly obvious," Jazzy observed. "Get it? Fair-ly obvious?"

"Got it." Trevor glanced at me. "Your cousin thinks she's pretty smart."

"I don't think," she corrected him. "I know."

"You don't think," Trevor repeated smugly. "I rest my case."

"No different from the girls you hang with, I bet," she shot back.

"How do you know who I hang with?" he demanded.

She smiled slyly at him. "I can tell."

"Just be glad that she's your first cousin," Trevor said to me. "First cousins can't get married!"

Jazzy tossed her black hair. "I'm *never* getting married."

They kept talking like that, words bouncing back and forth. With the sun on my head and Mom's food in my belly I couldn't think of anything to add to the conversation, so I stayed quiet. Clamming had turned my brain to mush.

When we got to the pond, Jazzy ran down to the water's edge. She crossed her arms, reached down to grab both sides of her tank top, and then pulled up, undressing in one graceful movement.

"What're you looking at?" she asked Trevor.

"Nothing." He laughed.

She was wearing a black one-piece bathing suit that was hard not to stare at. I don't know how else to say it: Jazzy had an amazing body. She sprinted to the water and dove in.

Trevor and I raced after her. The cool water felt like heaven on my sore arms and shoulders. Jazzy surfaced, shook back her hair, and went underwater again. Then she started stroking out away from the shore. I had to swim hard to keep up with her.

"You're fast," I said.

"Ho, he does speak!" Jazzy grinned. "Yeah, I'm on the swim team at school. Butterfly, free, and breast."

She squirted water out of her mouth. Trevor swam over to where we were treading water.

"I just remembered something I read," he said. "Some cultures do allow first cousins to marry. But you have to have genetic counseling, or something. Otherwise you might end up with a three-headed baby."

"That would be so cute!" Jazzy said, and she dove underwater.

I turned onto my back and stroked lazily toward shore. Jazzy and Trevor followed. After we dried off, Jazzy pulled out her camera and took a few pictures. A little ways off we could see three guys yelling and clowning around—Bird Shirsty, Ross Perelli, and Tommy O'Rourke, kids who went to my school. They were doing handstands at the edge of the water. Jazzy walked over and asked Ross to take a picture of me and Trevor, with her in the middle.

"Not a problem," Ross said, bowing like a butler. He snapped the photo and went back to his group.

"So how about that fair?" Jazzy said. "You guys gonna take me? Or do I have to go with somebody else?"

"Like who?" Trevor demanded.

"Ho, da cute!" Jazzy was staring at Tommy O'Rourke, a darkly tanned kid with long blond hair. "Who's that boy?"

"Tommy O'Rourke," I said. "He's a monster surfer."

"He's a mental midget but he's got a cool boat—a Chris Craft XK 19. He was telling me about it. It's red, with a white interior. But there's some dirt going 'round about Tommy." Trevor lowered his voice. "I heard he's been making tons of money this summer digging clams."

"Really?" I said. "I've never seen him on the bay."

Trevor lowered his voice. "I hear he's been digging in the cove."

Dan had warned me about the Babylon Cove where the clams were supposedly plentiful. But it was illegal to harvest them so close in; the clams were said to be polluted. If Conservation caught you, they would confiscate your boat, pull your clamming license, and hit you with a huge fine. But some guys were willing to take the risk. They went at night, driving sleek boats equipped with oversized engines, boats so fast they could outrun the Conservation boats.

"Who says he's been digging in the cove?" I asked.

"I've got my sources." He shrugged. "Anyway, when are you going to take me clamming? Huh?"

"You'd hate it."

"I'd love the money," he shot back.

"Hey, they don't just give it to you. I bust my butt out there."

"C'mon, Squire, take me clamming with you. I want to dig me some clams!"

Trevor flexed his muscles. I opened my mouth in an exaggerated yawn. "Sorry, Trev. I forgot to bring my magnifying glass."

After a while the sun turned hot, and the three of us went back into the water.

"Hey, Matt," Jazzy said. "Go over there for a sec."

I swam over to where she was pointing, and stood waiting in waist-deep water.

"Spread your legs," she told me. "Stand still."

Jazzy took a breath and submerged. Beneath the surface I could see her streaking toward me. She didn't touch me, but I did feel a pulse of energy—like electricity—as she passed through my legs.

COUNTY FAIR

THAT NIGHT Mom took Jazzy and me to the fairgrounds in West Islip. Trevor said his brother would drive us home. I bought two tickets, and we went through the entrance gate. The scene inside was wild and loud. Spotlights, big tents, balloons. Girls shrieking on rides. I smelled french fries, popcorn, cotton candy, fresh hay. Jazzy giggled at seeing a toddler with a candy apple—the kid's face was smeared with caramel.

Trevor came over to join us. He was with Allison, his on-and-off girlfriend.

"This is Jazzy, Matt's cousin," Trevor said. "She's from Hawaii."

"Yeah?" Allison's blue eyes grew wide. She was wearing a miniskirt and too much makeup for my taste. "Waikiki Beach?"

"I live about forty-five miles from there," Jazzy explained.

"Are you Hawaiian?" she asked.

"No, she's Martian." Trevor rolled his eyes.

"Hawaiian and some other stuff, half-half," Jazzy told Allison.

"I knew you were Hawaiian!" Allison cried. "I love your hair!"

Jazzy smiled. "Thanks."

"I saw this show on TV that said Hawaiian girls wear flowers in their hair," Allison said. "If you wear it on one side it means you're available to go out with a guy. But if you wear the flower on the other side it means you're already taken. Right?"

"How about it?" Trevor asked Jazzy. "Are you available or already taken?"

"Right now, I'm hungry," Jazzy replied. "C'mon, let's get something to eat."

"You want some cotton candy?" I asked.

"No, I want that." Jazzy pulled me over to the fried-dough booth. I motioned to the lady inside that I wanted one. With a long slotted spoon, she lifted a piece of golden dough out of bubbling oil. Then she sprinkled powdered sugar on top and handed it to me on a paper plate. The smell was driving me nuts. Jazzy broke off a piece and put it into her mouth.

"Mmm, that's so *ono*." She closed her eyes.

"Huh?" I asked.

"*Ono* means delicious in Hawaiian," Jazzy explained.

"Don't people ever share in Hawaii?" Trevor complained.

"Take it easy, boy!" Jazzy passed around the fried dough so we could all try it. "Hey, let's go on a ride, Matt. How about that one?"

She pointed at the roller coaster.

"No can do," I told her. "I always get sick on those spinning rides."

"Me, too," Allison admitted.

"You guys are pathetic!" Trevor shook his head. "C'mon, Jazzy!"

Jazzy handed me the plate of fried dough and ran off with Trevor. Together they boarded the ride. Allison and I stood watching the roller coaster shoot past. We could hear Trevor's maniacal laughter. Jazzy's eyes and mouth were open, her long hair fluttering like a black scarf behind her. Allison didn't take her eyes off them.

"She's so cool," Allison said.

"You think so?" I asked.

Allison nodded. I went to break a piece of the fried dough, but now it was cold and greasy. Jazzy and Trevor stumbled off the roller coaster and raced over to the spinning teacups.

Standing beside me, Allison shivered. Her shoulders were bare.

"Cold?" I asked.

"No." She slumped against the railing, looking glum. "Is your cousin going to be visiting long?"

"For the summer."

"Oh, really?" That news seemed to make Allison's mood even gloomier. She stood in silence, watching Trevor and Jazzy spin madly in their teacups.

"Totally insane," Trevor said when they got off the ride.

"That was fun!" Jazzy used my shoulder to steady herself. "You guys should try it."

"No thanks." Allison grabbed Trevor's hand and held on tight.

"How about you?" Jazzy asked me. "Can't you go on *any* rides?"

"Like maybe the merry-go-round?" Trevor suggested.

"C'mon!" Jazzy grabbed my hand and pulled me toward the Ferris wheel. There wasn't a line when we got there. The guy who operated the Ferris wheel had a long ponytail and a hard face. I saw him checking out Jazzy in an obvious way as she climbed into the compartment.

"Enjoy the ride, sweetheart." He was grinning as he locked us in.

"Idiot," I muttered.

"Why boddah you, eh?" Jazzy nudged me, laughing.

"Huh?" I looked at her.

"It's pidgin. 'Why boddah you' means, like, what do you care if that guy is checking me out?"

"Do you and your friends talk pidgin?" I asked.

"Sometimes," Jazzy said. "But you can't use pidgin in school or you'll get in trouble with the teachers."

The compartments got loaded one by one, notching us higher and higher into the night. It felt like we were climbing stairs into the sky. The higher we rose, the more lights we could see spread out below us. When we reached the very top, the Ferris wheel suddenly stopped. Jazzy took out her camera and snapped some pictures. We waited several minutes, but nothing happened.

"What's the problem?" I muttered.

"Whoa!" Jazzy dangled her feet in the air. "We're a long way up."

I couldn't look down.

"Afraid of heights?" she asked.

"A little," I admitted.

"Well, I'm not." For the first time, I noticed her eyes, big and brown. "I'm not afraid of anything."

When the ride ended we walked over to the arcade.

"Hey, look at that!" Jazzy pointed at a row of gigantic stuffed puppies, Saint Bernards, in one of the booths. "Look at that cutie! Can you win that for me, Matt?"

The booth was for shooting a BB gun at a target.

"Honestly? No."

"Aw, c'mon, try!" Jazzy urged.

Behind the counter was an old woman with a cigarette between her lips and a voice like rough sandpaper. "Two bucks for three shots. You gotta get two in the dark center circle."

It seemed like a waste of my clamming money, but everyone was looking at me, so I pulled two dollars from my wallet and gave it to her.

"Here goes nothing," Trevor said.

"Shush!" Allison told him.

I lined up the barrel and pulled the trigger. Trevor laughed. My shot didn't even hit the target.

"You have to steady the gun," Jazzy said. She showed me how to rest my elbows on the counter. Then she cushioned the stock of the barrel against my cheek. "Don't pull the trigger, squeeze it. Take a breath, let out half of it, and squeeze the trigger, okay?"

"Okay," I said. This time my shot hit the target, about two inches to the left of the dark center spot.

"Yeah!" Jazzy exclaimed.

My next shot was even closer. The old woman gave me one of the small puppies, which was about three inches tall.

"Sorry it's not the big one," I said, handing it to Jazzy. But she looked delighted and gave the dog a hug.

"*Mahalo!* Thanks, Matt! Now, my turn."

Jazzy took the gun into her arms. All three of her shots hit the first ring from the bull's-eye. The lady gave her a dog twice the size of the one I'd won. Jazzy put the two stuffed dogs together.

"Now the puppy has a mother!" she said and smiled.

A half hour later, Trevor's big brother, Raymond, showed up to drive us home. When Jazzy and I walked into the house, the kitchen was empty.

"How come you know so much about shooting a gun?"

"My uncle taught me. Look."

A photograph was lying on the kitchen table. Jazzy picked it up and let out a squeal of laughter. The picture showed two small kids, maybe two or three years old, standing in a plastic pool, both stark naked. There was a sticky note attached to the photo: "Look at you two in your birthday suits!"

"Oh my God—is that really . . . us?" Jazzy asked in a high-pitched voice.

I felt kind of embarrassed with Jazzy standing there looking at that photograph.

"I was taller than you then," she pointed out.

"Not anymore." I moved closer to show that now I had a good two inches on her.

"Tired?" she asked.

"These days I'm always tired." I said goodnight and staggered off to bed.

ELECTRICAL STORM

TUESDAY MORNING, I got a surprise: Trevor showed up at the dock.

"Who are you?" Dan asked from the bow of the *Morrison Hotel.*

"I'm Trevor, a friend of Matt's. I thought maybe you wouldn't mind if I came clamming with you guys. I won't—"

"You thought wrong." Dan shook his head. "If you're looking for a ferryboat, go over to Captree Boat Basin. This is a clam boat. C'mon, Matt. Let's roll."

Trevor and I swapped a quick look before I stepped onto the boat. Dan fired up the engine. I felt kind of sorry for Trevor, standing at the dock as our boat began moving down the canal.

I could see that Dan was in a bad mood, so I stayed clear of him. He worked his side of the boat, I worked mine. Digging clams doesn't require much brain work, which left my mind free to wander. I pictured my dad in Montana. The Boston Whaler I was going to buy. Jazzy at the top of the Ferris wheel. The look on her face when I won that stuffed puppy for her.

By lunch, I'd been quiet for two solid hours, and the silence was starting to get on my nerves.

"I need to ask you something," I finally said. "What's the big deal about the cove?"

Dan shot me a suspicious look. "What about it?"

"Is it true what they say?" I asked. "That it's loaded with clams?"

"Here's all you need to know about the cove." Dan leaned back and wiped his mouth. "Number one: it's illegal to clam there. Number two: Conservation won't fool around if they catch you in there. You get cute and try to outrun those guys, they'll pull out a rifle and shoot a bullet through your engine block. Any more questions?"

"Did you fight in the Vietnam War?" I asked.

"That's right. Fifteen months." He stuffed his trash back into his lunch bag. "It's not my favorite subject, okay?"

"Okay."

When I got home from clamming, I heard an unfamiliar sound: music. I followed the sound to the den. Jazzy was sitting at the edge of the easy chair, playing guitar. Mom sat on the couch, listening attentively. Jazzy sang:

I sat on your lap
and strummed your guitar.
You taught me my first chord,
said I'd be a music star.

I'll never forget your voice, your voice,
I'll never forget your eyes;
I'll never forget your laugh, your laugh,
I'll never forget your smile.

Her face had a dreamy look as she sang. The guitar sounded strong and clear, but it was Jazzy's voice that surprised me most. I'd never heard anyone sing like her.

You called me Jazzy-girl;
I called you Daddy-bear.
I thought of you this mor-ning,
combing out my hair.

I'll never forget your voice, your voice,
I'll never forget your eyes;
I'll never forget your laugh, your laugh,
I'll never forget your smile.

When the song ended, Mom had tears in her eyes. "That's lovely, Jazzy," she said softly.

"Thanks, Aunt Alice. I really hoped you'd like it."

"Such a tribute to my brother. You've got an amazing voice."

Jazzy smiled. "I've always loved to sing, even when I was little."

"Yeah, it sounded great," I agreed. "How long have you been playing?"

"Since I was about ten or eleven. Mom got me lessons and I sort of took to it." Jazzy bent her head to tune one of the strings. "Mom says music's in my blood."

That night I awoke from a deep sleep. Thunder! I opened my eyes just in time to see my room illuminated an instant before a huge thunderclap shook the house. Then it was like a dream: My bedroom door opened and a ghostly figure entered.

Jazzy.

She stood there in her white nightgown. After a few seconds, I saw her mouth move, but a growl of thunder drowned her words. She came to the side of my bed. I sat up.

"I'm scared," she whispered. "I knocked on your mother's door, but I don't think she heard me."

"What's wrong?" I asked her.

"Lightning." When she leaned toward me, her long hair dangled onto my bed. "My best friend got hit by lightning.

She was in the hospital for weeks. Since then, lightning really scares me. Can I . . . stay here . . . just for a few minutes?"

I didn't say anything, but she must have taken my silence as a yes because she quickly climbed into bed and pulled up the covers. I turned to the wall. She slid closer and huddled against me, trembling something fierce. "Thanks," she whispered.

I wasn't wearing any shirt, and I could feel her long hair slide down my back. I think I started trembling, too. I just tried to breathe, in and out.

The room lit up again. More thunder. *Crack!* Jazzy made a soft sound, like a whimper, and pulled herself tighter against me.

Bang! Bang! Bang! It almost sounded like . . . knocking. Then I made out the outline of a person.

Mom. She walked in and switched on the light.

"This isn't your bed," Mom said to Jazzy.

"I know." Jazzy sat up and swallowed a sob. "I'm sorry . . . I, uh, I'm so scared of lightning."

Jazzy started telling the story of how her best friend got zapped by lightning, but Mom raised her hand. Jazzy fell silent. Mom stared at me.

"What?" I asked.

"What?" Mom repeated angrily. "What?"

Jazzy got out of bed and started to leave, but Mom stopped her.

"Wait." She looked at me. "How long has this been going on?"

"What?"

She pointed at my bed. "*This.*"

"Nothing's going on," I told her. "She was scared of the storm so she came in."

She looked at me skeptically. "Can you look me in the eyes and tell me you two aren't . . . messing around?"

"We're not!" Now I was the one getting mad.

"I was scared," Jazzy insisted, looking at Mom. "I knocked on your door, but you didn't answer."

There was another bolt of lightning, followed by a loud, guttural roar.

"I think the storm's just about over," Mom said. "Come on, Jazzy. If you want, you can sleep with me tonight."

Mom nodded at me and turned off the light as she left. In the darkness I could hear the storm moving east past Blue Point and Patchogue, heading toward the Hamptons. The thunder faded, replaced by the sound of heavy rain. For a couple of minutes I just lay there, motionless. When I moved my feet to one side, the bottom sheet was still warm where Jazzy had been lying.

SLOW JAZZ

MOM APOLOGIZED the next morning while she fixed my sandwiches for lunch. I sat at the table, eating cereal with raisins and sliced bananas.

"Guess I overreacted a little, huh?" she said.

I didn't answer.

"Okay, so maybe I overreacted a lot," she admitted. "It's new for me, Matt, having a girl in the house. I'd feel responsible with any relative visiting, but with a girl it's even . . . more so. Anyway, I'm sorry if it seemed like I was accusing you. I guess I'm a bit jumpy."

"It's okay, Mom." I'd already forgiven her.

That day, while I dug clams, I thought about Jazzy. I couldn't help it. She was smart, strong, beautiful, and different from any of the girls I knew at school. I had never thought of her as anything except my seldom-seen cousin from Hawaii. As I stood amidst the piles of bay muck, pieces from last night floated back to me. The brilliant flashes of light in my bed-room. The way the storm made Jazzy tremble. The silky-soft feel of her long hair sliding down my back.

At supper, Mom announced that she and Jazzy were going back to the fair.

"Why don't you come with us?" Mom said.

"Yeah, come," Jazzy urged.

"I'm too tired," I moaned.

"They're going to have a greased-pig contest," Mom said. "And cow-plop bingo. That's always a spectacle."

"I'm wiped," I said. "Sorry."

After Mom and Jazzy left, I stretched out on my bed. It was a hot, humid night, but my room felt cool. I said a prayer of thanks to the god of air-conditioning before I fell asleep.

I woke to voices in the kitchen. I looked at my clock: 11:09 p.m. I realized it was Mom and Jazzy coming back from the fair. For a few minutes I lay there, listening but unable to make out what they were talking about. Soon I heard Mom and Jazzy say goodnight. Then I heard a soft rustling—rain. It was a cozy sound, and I closed my eyes to go back to sleep, but I felt too awake. Pulling on my jeans and T-shirt, I went to the den. Jazzy was leaning over a legal pad, writing.

"Oh, hi," she said, looking up. "Did we wake you?"

I went to the window. "I think it was the rain."

"It just started a few minutes ago." Jazzy came and stood next to me. Her left arm brushed mine.

"Can't sleep?" I asked.

"Nope. Guess I'm still on Hawaiian time."

"You worried about another thunderstorm?" I asked.

"No."

I couldn't resist teasing her. "I thought you said you're not afraid of anything."

"Yeah . . . well . . . sorry about barging into your room like that." She smiled at me. "I won't do that again. I almost got you in trouble."

"It's okay." I shrugged. "How was the fair? Did you see Trevor?"

She nodded. "He was with Allison. Isn't that girl a little . . . insecure? She wouldn't let him out of her sight for a second. Oh, and we saw those kids who were at the pond. What's his name? Tommy O'Rourke? Yeah, and his friends."

We stood listening to the rain, which was falling harder now. I thought of Dan's boat getting drenched at the dock. By tomorrow the wooden decks would be shiny clean.

"Maybe you won't have to work tomorrow," she murmured.

"I doubt it." Right then I couldn't imagine anything better than sleeping late on a rainy morning. But Dan struck me as the kind of guy who would go clamming in a typhoon. "Were you writing a letter?"

"No, I'm working on a new song. Hey, I want you to hear something."

She went to her room and came back a moment later with a record album. She slid it halfway out of its jacket.

"Can we bring your record player out to the porch?"

The porch was dark and noisy with rain. Jazzy put the album on the turntable. She plugged in a pair of headphones and lifted them to my ears.

"Listen," she whispered.

What I heard was music, I guess, though it didn't sound like any music I knew. Mostly it was a bunch of raw, wild, loud, fast, frantic, bee-bee-beeping, bop-bop-bopping sounds, a crazy traffic jam of hurried horns and drums and guitars. Jazzy lifted the headphones off.

"That's some juicing jazz, yah?"

"Shh," I said. "We need to be quiet or else we'll wake up Mom."

"Whoops, sorry," she whispered. "So what do you think about that jazz?"

"I'm getting a headache," I told her.

She looked disappointed. "That's Charlie Parker. You don't like it?"

"Sorry." I handed her the headphones.

"Wait."

She lifted the needle and changed records. This time what hit my ears was a soft, rich sound. Mellow piano. Brushes hitting a drum in slow rhythm. And behind it all, the bass, like a big powerful heart, beating in the exact center of the music. She put the headphones on me again.

"How's that?" she mouthed.

"Better," I mouthed back. The music had a melancholy quality that was perfect for a rainy night. She lifted the headphones off my ears.

"That's a different kind of jazz," she whispered. "Can you hear the bass? That's what my father used to play. I've got this great picture of him reaching around the instrument to finger the strings. Like he and his bass are slow-dancing."

Jazzy fitted the headphones back around my head. Then she put her arms around me, which was the last thing I expected. I felt her fingers moving up and down the middle of my back, as if my spine was one of the strings on a stand-up bass. After the shock faded, I noticed how good it felt to have her holding me. Actually, great. Her hair smelled so sweet that I got the urge to kiss her, a really strong urge, and I might have done that except for the voice in my head that kept reminding me, *She's your first cousin.* . . .

So I didn't kiss her. Didn't cross that line. But I didn't push her away, either. We stood like that for a while, rocking back and forth in the dark, slow-dancing to that easy jazz.

Too soon, the song ended. Jazzy looked up and smiled. When she took the headphones from my ears I could hear the rain again, coming down harder than ever. Jazzy turned and went back into the house. A minute later I went to my room, turned off the light, and closed my eyes. But I knew sleep wouldn't come easy.

RiGHTY TiGHTY, LEFTY LOOSY

I'D ASKED DAN for a day off. Jazzy was itching to see the ocean, so Mom took us to Robert Moses beach on Fire Island. Mom's friend Peg came along, too. They set up beach chairs so they could dangle their feet in the surf. Jazzy stood, shading her eyes, gazing toward the water.

"Nice beach, huh?" I asked.

She frowned, crinkling her nose. "Tell you the truth, I thought the water would be a lot more blue."

I laughed. "C'mon, I'll race you."

We sprinted toward the water. Jazzy was as fast as me, but the moment she touched the water she spun back in alarm.

"It's freezing!"

Watching from her beach chair, Mom laughed. "I guess the ocean is warmer in Hawaii, huh?"

"Much!" Jazzy hugged herself fiercely. "Matt, next time we go to the beach can you warm up the ocean first?"

"I'll get right on it," I promised.

It didn't take her long to get used to the water. There was a line of decent-sized waves rearing up and breaking fifty feet offshore, and we had a great time bodysurfing. When we got back to our blanket, Jazzy started combing out her hair. She took two lemons and cut them each in half.

"What are you doing?"

Ignoring me, Jazzy scooted to the edge of her towel, leaned back, and squeezed juice from one of the halves into her hair. "Lemon juice. It helps to lighten your hair."

"Why don't you just bleach it so you can be blond like Allison?"

"Nope." She combed the juice through her long hair. "I just want to make my hair a little lighter. It's so black."

"You're pretty good at bodysurfing," I said. "Can you surf on a regular surfboard?"

"I can surf, play the ukulele, and dance the hula. A real Hawaiian girl," she said with a smile.

"Hula? You lie."

"It's true."

"When are you going to let me see you dance the hula?"

She laughed and flopped onto her towel. "You pretty optimistic, boy!"

"You should've brought your guitar," I said, stretching out my towel.

"I'd feel like a hippie," she murmured, "playing guitar on the beach."

"You got hippies in Hawaii?"

"Plenty. Last month I went with my friends to the beach and saw these hippie guys. They were standing on their heads watching the sunrise! I think those hippies had been smoking some *pakalolo*. That's what we call marijuana."

It turned out to be a nice day. We stayed at the beach until after four. When we got home, the weather was still so nice that Mom decided to have a cookout. All that swimming and riding waves made me hungry; I don't think burgers off the grill ever tasted so good.

Next morning I found Mom at the kitchen with the newspaper open in front of her.

"This Watergate scandal keeps getting worse and worse," she said, showing me the front page. "Look."

NIXON ORDERS SECRET SERVICE
NOT TO TESTIFY ABOUT WIRETAPPING

"They're a bunch of crooks, every last one of them." Mom shook her head. "These days the crossword puzzle is the only thing in the paper that doesn't get me mad. Matt, I'm stuck on this one. Who's the 'Say Hey Kid'? It starts with *W*."

"Willie Mays," I replied. He was my favorite player. "Does that fit?"

"Like a baseball glove." She laughed at her own bad joke.

"Is Jazzy still sleeping?" I asked.

"I think so."

I noticed that Mom was already dressed. "Are you going to church?"

"There's a nine o'clock. I'll say a prayer for you." She smiled. "It can't hurt."

"Why do you go, Mom?"

"I don't know." She went to the counter and tucked my sandwiches and some chips into a lunch bag. "I guess it just makes me feel better, inside and out."

I nodded, even though I had an odd feeling about the whole church thing. At first Dad, Mom, and I used to attend mass only on Sundays, like most people. Then I noticed that Mom would drive to church two or three times during the week. Sometimes I wondered if maybe all that churchgoing was part of what made Dad move out. When Dad left, I stopped going. Mom said I didn't have to go if I didn't want to. And I didn't.

At lunch Dan tossed me a peach, but he didn't have much to say. When Bert arrived, he started looking for food on my side of the boat, which struck me as funny—the pile of clams, crabs, and muck on Dan's side was at least three times bigger than mine.

The One O'Clock Chop came on schedule, but this time the wind kept blowing harder and harder. Pretty soon I could feel our boat straining at the anchor. Small whitecaps appeared on the open bay. The boat swayed back and forth, making it almost impossible to handle the tongs. By quitting time I'd dug only a half bushel, Dan had barely dug two, and we were both in a bad mood when I went to pull the anchor.

As Dan tugged the starter cord, the Evinrude made a funny sound. It sputtered, coughed, and revved loudly before it conked out. Dan swore and removed the engine casing. He checked the plugs, unscrewed the fuel line, and fiddled with the choke. Then he tried again to start the engine. Nothing.

"We're drifting," I said. The wind was pushing us south toward Fire Island. We always had a certain amount of bilge water in our boat; now as the *Morrison Hotel* rocked I could feel the water washing back and forth below the deck. "And I think we're taking on water."

"Bilge pump needs to be tightened," Dan said. "I meant to do it this morning. You'll need to tighten the screws on all four sides."

"Me?"

"You." He handed me a screwdriver. "The bilge is under there."

I went into the cabin and climbed down below the steering wheel. In the dim light I found the bilge pump. It was hard to position myself with the boat rocking, the bilge water sloshing, and hardly any room to maneuver. I had no choice but to lower my hands into that disgusting water. Groping around, I found the four screws the bilge pump was mounted on. But which way to turn them? *Righty tighty, lefty loosy*, I remembered, and tightened the screws.

"Fixed it," I said when I emerged from the cabin. Bending down, I washed the bilge water off my hands and forearms. Dan switched on the pump, and it started pumping us out. But we were still drifting. The chop was blowing us like a sail.

"Maybe someone will stop to help us," I said.

"Don't hold your breath." Dan shook his head. "Eighty percent of the people in this world don't care about the problems you've got. And the other 20 percent are glad you've got them."

"I don't believe that," I said after a moment.

"Oh you don't, huh?" He glared at me. "Give me my screwdriver."

I handed it to him. *Righty tighty, lefty loosy*. My father had taught me that. In fact, I remembered the exact moment when he spoke those words. We were in our garage, working side by side, making a car for the Soap Box Derby when I was a Boy Scout. Funny, whenever I thought of him in Montana, I pictured him living alone, without Heather. I knew he played the stock market, and he made at least two trips to Las Vegas every year, to gamble. My father was no saint, but at that moment I missed him a lot.

I noticed a boat approaching, a Garvey like ours.

"Need help?" the driver yelled when he got close enough. Dan was too disgusted to answer. When the other boat came alongside, I threw our bowline to him. The man cut his engine and tied our line to his stern.

"Do you know what's wrong?" The man stepped onto our boat and looked at the Evinrude. He was a lot leaner than Dan, but he looked strong in a lanky kind of way.

"Not a clue," Dan said, lifting his meaty shoulders. "It ran perfect this morning. The plugs are brand-new."

"You got any Drygas?" the man asked. "Some of the marinas around here have been selling gas with water in it."

He gave Dan a small plastic container. Dan opened it and poured the Drygas into the engine. Then he pulled the starter cord and it fired right up. Heavy white smoke poured out, but at least it was running.

"Let it run a minute or so," the man yelled over the roar.

"Thanks." Dan pulled out his wallet, but the guy shook his head.

"Next time it might be me needing you," he said, stepping back onto his boat. We kept our engine running, just in case. I was trying like crazy not to smile. When the other boat cast off, Dan swiveled his big head and shot me a murderous look.

"Don't say it, kid. I'm not in the mood today. Understand?"

I understood. He cranked the music, and we headed in.

The next morning I couldn't move my right hand. It was strange and frightening—I could move the whole arm just fine, but my fingers and thumb were knotted together, clenched in a frozen fist. My alarm was beeping, but I wasn't able to extend a finger to shut it off.

What was happening? Was my hand paralyzed? I'd seen a movie involving a mysterious virus, with people getting twisted into grotesque shapes before they died a horrible death. It hit me—maybe I've got arthritis, like Mom. I staggered out of bed and opened my door.

"Mom!" I yelled. I was panicking and didn't care who I woke up. Jazzy's door opened. She stood in her white nightgown, rubbing her eyes. Mom hurried into my bedroom.

"My hand!" I told her. "It won't open!"

Mom took my hand in hers and tried to lift my forefinger, but it wouldn't move.

"Don't!" I cried.

"Does it hurt?"

"No, but I can't move it! What's wrong, Mom?"

She closed her eyes to think. "I'll call the clinic, though I doubt anyone will be in this early."

As she hurried toward the kitchen, Jazzy came across the hallway. She led me back to my bed, like I was a child. When she took my hand in hers I smelled something sweet.

"What's that?"

"Coconut oil," she explained. "This stuff will cure anything." She began massaging me with the oil, first my arm, then lower, to my wrist, kneading the muscles under the skin. She had strong hands, and she took her time, working slow and steady.

"What if I've got some kind of killer virus?"

"Try to hang loose. You know the Hawaiian sign for that, right?" Jazzy shook her right hand, waggling her thumb and pinky.

"I can't 'hang loose'! My hand is paralyzed!"

"Listen, you're going to be okay, okay?" Jazzy sounded so calm and sure of herself, I closed my eyes and tried to make myself relax. Luckily, all my toes moved when I tried to wiggle them. At least the rest of my body was working.

Mom appeared in the doorway. All at once I felt something loosen in my hand. My fingers moved! One by one—pinky, ring, middle, pointer, and thumb—they stretched open. I made a fist, opened it, and made another fist. The hand felt stiff and creaky.

"Thank heavens!" Mom let out a sigh of relief. "You okay?"

"Yeah." I took a deep breath and looked up at Jazzy. "Thanks."

She grinned. "Now you're perfect."

DAVY JONES'S LOCKER

WHEN MOM AND JAZZY drove me to the dock it was smothered in thick fog. The boats looked ghostly at their moorings, shrouded in mist. Dan was loading our clam tongs onto his boat.

"Who's Hercules?" Jazzy asked.

"That's my boss, Dan. Thanks for dropping me off, Mom. See you guys later."

Mom and Jazzy waved as we motored slowly down the canal. Dan drove cautiously, standing and peering ahead. Usually he gunned the engine when we reached the open bay; today he nudged it to half speed. I went to the back of the boat and told Dan what had happened to my hand on Saturday.

"Just a cramp," he said. "Used to happen to me a lot when I first started clamming. No big deal."

Twenty-five minutes later I tossed the anchor overboard. The mist was still so thick we couldn't see more than thirty feet in any direction. It was eerie. I knew that other clammers were anchored nearby, because we could hear their grunts, soft curses, the banging of the tongs, and the clatter of clams on wooden decks. It was strange to hear all that when we couldn't see them. The clammers stayed a half hour before they pulled anchor and left.

Dan's silence plus the thick fog made me feel even more alone, but that was fine with me. I wanted to be alone so I could think about what had happened that morning in my room. I kept replaying the scene in my head: that weird paralysis, the smell of coconut oil, the way Jazzy had rubbed my cramped hand and made it come alive. I wouldn't have believed it if I hadn't seen and felt it myself.

"Sun should burn off this crap soon," Dan said. But we stayed socked in all morning and ate lunch in the fog. It felt like being lost in a desert, or the middle of a blizzard, with no landmarks, nothing but white as far as we could see on all sides.

At around one forty-five I threw in my tongs and hit something. I pulled them up, trying to untangle them from whatever it was, but they didn't come clean and I couldn't shake it off. Finally, I gave up and lifted the tongs, letting the caught object come up slowly with them. Whatever it was, it was heavy.

Staring down, I saw it. A shoe.

A pair of black pants.

"Dan!" I yelled.

"What?"

I pointed. The body of a man, fully clothed, was floating on his belly beside the boat. Dan cursed loudly.

"How the—"

"My tongs got caught and I—"

"Look out!" he said. "I'm gonna pull him up."

Dan reached under the body and lifted, straining with all his might. The boat started tipping.

"Stand over there," he gasped, motioning to the starboard side. I moved to the other side of the boat to counterbalance the mass of the waterlogged body, which must've weighed a ton. Somehow Dan managed to wrestle it onto our boat. I came over to get a closer view, but Dan blocked my path.

"Don't look," he ordered, breathing hard. He went into the cabin to get something. I didn't know where to put my eyes, so I just stared at the horizon and tried to calm my thumping heart. Dan came out, leaned over the body, and went back to the cabin. Through the glass I could see him talking on his radio.

"I'm calling to report a dead male. . . . Yes, dead as in deceased! . . . Do I need to spell that? . . . Yeah, I'm on a white Garvey, about a mile west of the causeway bridge. . . . Yeah, Robert Moses. . . . Maybe three quarters of a mile south. . . . Hard to say in the fog. . . . Not far from the yacht club. . . . All right. . . . All right. . . . Yeah, all right, fine, I ain't going anywhere. . . ."

He came out of the cabin and looked at me. "Coast Guard should be here in twenty minutes, if they can find us in this soup."

I turned around. Dan had covered the dead man's face from the nose up with a white rag.

"Why'd you do that?" I asked.

"The eyes are gone," he explained. "That's the first thing the crabs eat when you go down to Davy Jones's Locker."

I wasn't eager to see that. Stepping closer, I looked at the lower half of the man's face. I'd never seen a dead body before, and the drowned corpse looked pretty gruesome— the too-white skin, the man's tongue hanging out like a strip of wide, soggy ribbon. There was a strand of seaweed on the chin. I stared at the mouth. The blue lips actually moved! Could this man possibly be alive? Trying to speak? Then I was horrified to see the lips part. An eel slithered out of the man's mouth, green, about eight inches long. Dan swore,

stomped on it, and kicked it overboard, but my knees buck-
led and I threw up over the side.

"That's all right," Dan said. For a second I thought he was
going to put his big hand—the hand that had touched the
corpse—on the back of my neck. Looking down into the
water, I felt the nausea rise and threw up again.

Dan handed me his thermos of ice water. After I drank, I
pressed it against my cheek and forced myself to take four
deep breaths.

"Feel better?" he asked.

"I think so." I stood up, still feeling pretty wobbly.

"Take it easy," Dan said. "This guy hasn't been dead too
long. I'd guess a day, maybe less."

"How can you tell?"

"I don't know. Looks pretty good for a dead guy, don't you
think?" Dan reached into the man's pocket and pulled out
his wallet. "Raymond Grillo. The guy's just a year younger
than me."

The radio crackled in the cabin. Dan went back to answer
the call. A minute later he came out carrying a small horn.

"Cover your ears," he told me. The horn gave an ear-
splitting *blattt*. He did that three more times before the Coast
Guard ship finally appeared in the fog, steaming toward us.
Three uniformed guys boarded the *Morrison Hotel*. After

quick introductions, the men began to examine the body. One guy peeled off Dan's towel to examine the head. I made a point of not looking. The tallest man whipped out a pad of paper and asked me some questions.

"How long have you been digging clams with your father?"

"He's not my father."

"Oh, sorry." The man glanced over at Dan. "Friend of the family?"

"Something like that," Dan replied.

"You live with your parents?"

"My mother."

"Where did you find the body, Matt?"

"I was tonging, right over here. I felt something."

"When was that?"

"About a half hour ago."

"One forty-five," Dan told the man.

"You called the Coast Guard right away?" the man asked Dan.

"Yeah. I found this in the guy's pocket. The man's name is Raymond Grillo. Lives in Lido Beach."

Dan tossed the wallet to the tall guy. The man examined it closely. "This is important evidence," the man told Dan. "Did you remove anything from it?"

"Nope."

The tall guy looked at me. "See anything unusual this morning? Anything at all?"

"No. We couldn't see much of anything with this fog."

"Okay, that's it for now. I've got both your phone numbers, in case we have more questions." He handed us each a business card. "Take this in case you need to get in touch with me."

It took the three men plus Dan, all straining like mules, to lift the man onto a stretcher and into the Coast Guard boat. We watched their boat depart. Our deck was dry except for the spot under Raymond Grillo's body where fluid had leaked out of him. I dumped five buckets of water onto that spot; Dan used the stiff-bristled broom to scrub the deck clean.

"Fog's lifting," he said.

Looking up, I could see that he was right. The fog was tearing apart in big, ragged pieces, letting in shafts of bright sunlight.

"You okay, Matt?"

"Yeah, I think so."

"You lie like a politician." He smiled at me. "Pull the anchor, kid. I'm going to take you home."

I didn't argue. On the way back to the docks I sat on the front of the bow, just letting the wind blow past my face.

Even with my eyes closed I kept seeing Raymond Grillo, his left hand sprawled on the deck. The gold Rolex watch. Fingers already frozen with rigor mortis. Fingers that no amount of coconut oil or massage or Hawaiian magic could ever bring back to life.

THE SALT LICK

MOM WAS SURPRISED to see me home so early. While Dan talked with Mom, I went to the bathroom, stripped off my clothes, and got into the shower. I made the water as hot as I could stand it, shampooed my hair twice, and carefully washed my body from head to toe. When I came out, my skin tingled. I dressed, threw the clothes I'd worn for work into the washing machine, and went to the kitchen.

Mom hugged me, pulling me tight against her. I couldn't seem to return her hug. I felt a little dead myself.

"My God, Matt," Jazzy said. "That must have been awful!"

I nodded. "It was. Did Dan leave?"

"Yes." Taking both my hands, Mom looked up at me. "Tell me what happened, Matt. I want to hear the whole thing."

So I sat down at the kitchen table and told them. I didn't leave out a single detail.

"The guy's eyes had been eaten away," I explained.

"Ugh!" Jazzy made a face and looked at Mom.

"But the worst thing was when the guy's mouth started moving," I said. "For a second I thought he might actually be alive, but then his mouth opened and an eel crawled out."

"Gross!" Jazzy said, horrified.

"That's when I threw up."

Mom squeezed my hand. "Why don't you go relax? Maybe take a nap?"

"Yeah, okay." I lay down on my bed. But when I closed my eyes, all I could see was the image of Raymond Grillo. I was way too wired to sleep, so I picked up the phone and punched in some digits.

"Aurora Insurance." It was Mrs. Jacobsen, my father's secretary. "May I help you?"

"This is Matt Carter. Could I please speak to my father?"

"Oh, hello, Matt," she said. "Right now he's on another call. Hang on, he shouldn't be long. Oops, wait, here he is."

"Hi, Matt! This is a nice surprise!" Dad's voice sounded strong and clear, like he was right next door. I had to remind myself that the words were being threaded all the way from Montana.

"Hi, Dad."

"How's it going? How's it feel to be living the life of a clam digger?"

"It's pretty hard, but I'm getting used to it."

"Heather makes a mean clam chowder," he said. "When you come visit, bring some clams with you. You can pack them in ice. Anyway, I'm proud of you, Matt. You've got a man's job. Your mother says you're making good money, too. You—"

"Dad," I interrupted. "Something happened today."

"What?"

"We were digging this morning and . . . well . . . I pulled up a dead guy."

Long pause. "Pulled him up? How?"

"With my clam tongs."

"You what? Did you say a dead guy?"

"His name was Raymond Grillo. The police say it looks like he drowned."

"Start at the beginning, Matt. What happened?"

So I told the story, beginning to end, for the second time.

"My God," he said when I finished. "You must be shell-shocked."

"Yeah, I guess I am."

He let out a long, hissing breath. "Listen, is your mother there?"

"Yeah."

"I want to speak with her. We need to make plans for your visit. When you come out, I'm going to barbecue us some steaks, thick as your fist. You haven't gone veggie on me, have you?"

"No." He was trying to cheer me up by changing the subject, but I wasn't ready to be cheered up yet.

"I've got tons of things planned," he was saying. "They don't have major-league baseball in Montana, but the fishing is fantastic. I found a great stream that's never crowded. We'll catch us a bunch of rainbow trout—I guarantee it, okay? I bought you some fly-fishing gear. Heather probably won't be able to get away, so it would be just you and me, camping out, like old times. You'd have to put up with me playing off-key Bob Dylan songs on the harmonica. But you're used to that by now."

"Yeah," I admitted.

"Hang in there, Matt," he said. "I'll call you tomorrow, see how you're doing. Now let me talk to your mother."

I had wanted to call my father because I thought talking with him would make me feel better, but I suddenly felt more drained than I'd ever been in my life. After I handed the phone to Mom I curled up on the bed and closed my eyes.

I fell into a dream. I was with Dad at Yankee Stadium. The seventh-inning stretch. Everyone stood and sang "Take Me Out to the Ball Game," and Dad sang louder than anyone, spreading his arms wide at the end: "old ballllllll gammmmmmmmme!"

"Who was better, Dad?" I asked when we sat down. "Joe DiMaggio or Ted Williams?"

"Honestly, I'm not sure," he told me. "You can make the case either way. But I'll give you a dollar bill if you can spell Carl Yastrzemski!"

He laughed and looked at me. But at that moment Dad's face turned into Dan's face. Then I felt someone shaking my shoulder. I opened my eyes. Mom.

"What time is it?" I asked, blinking.

"Six thirty," she answered.

"In the morning?"

She smiled. "Evening. Supper time. How're you feeling?"

"Better." I got up and splashed cold water on my face. My appetite had returned, too. Jazzy had fixed beef stew over rice, and it tasted great.

After dinner, we did the dishes and I helped Mom finish the crossword. Then I looked at the clock and went into the den, where Jazzy was strumming her guitar.

"It's eight thirty," I said, "so you know what that means. Time for *Hawaii Five-O!*"

"Mind if we turn it on?" Mom asked Jazzy as she came into the room.

"It's my favorite show!" Jazzy said, putting down the guitar.

We leaned forward as the *Hawaii Five-O* theme song started playing. The opening credits showed a giant curling wave breaking on the ocean, quickly followed by a picture of Jack Lord.

"Mr. Cool," I said.

"That's the Ilikai Hotel. . . . That's Aloha Tower. . . . And that's Diamond Head," Jazzy said. She shivered with excitement. "My friends and I love to watch and see if they show places we know. One day they showed my cousin Nani, just walking down the street."

"It's so beautiful." Mom sighed. "I hope watching this doesn't make you homesick."

Jazzy smiled. "It's a good show, but it's not very realistic. I mean, look at those guys wearing suits and ties. You think men walking around Honolulu dress like that? It's way too hot!"

At nine thirty the show ended and Mom went to bed. After that long nap, I didn't feel the least bit sleepy. Jazzy, too, seemed wide awake so we sat at the kitchen table and talked.

"Since I've been here my clock has been all backwards," she said. "I sleep in the day and stay up at night."

"Like a raccoon."

"Raccoons are cute," she said.

"They're also super-clean," I replied. "They wash everything with water before they eat it."

"Hey, you don't have to tell me about raccoons." Jazzy's hair swished back and forth. "I did a raccoon report in sixth grade, and I remember."

"I did a raccoon report in sixth grade," I mimicked, smiling at her. "You're going to tell me you got an A+, right?"

"As a matter of fact, I did."

We were both speaking in a near-whisper so we wouldn't disturb Mom.

"Isn't there somewhere we can go to talk?" she asked. "How about the porch?"

"I know a better place," I said. "C'mon."

I opened the back door; Jazzy slipped out with me. There's a path from our back yard that leads to four acres of woods behind our house. A big moon made it easy for us to find our way. The path went through the woods and emptied into a clearing about thirty feet across.

"Watch out," I said, pointing. It felt good to be able to speak in a normal voice. "That's springwater over there, and it's wicked cold."

Jazzy was wearing her puka-shell necklace. In the moonlight it glowed against her skin. She walked up to what looked like a small anvil set on a stand about chest high. "What's that?"

"I'll give you five dollars if you can guess."

"I have no idea."

"Taste it," I told her.

She looked at me like I was crazy, but she leaned forward and gave it a lick.

"Hey!"

"It's an old salt lick," I explained. "This land used to be pasture. I guess cows need lots of salt. And water. So they'd come here."

Jazzy licked it again. "Mmm, I love salt."

I bent down to the spring and put my hand all the way in, right up to my elbow. The water made me gasp. Jazzy came to stand next to me. She lowered her big toe into the water.

"Man! That's ice!"

"Comes out of the deepest part of the earth," I told her. "It never warms up."

As she twisted away Jazzy stumbled. I reached out to grab her hand so she wouldn't fall. She got her balance but didn't let go.

"It must have been weird, finding that dead guy," Jazzy said. "I've never seen a dead person. If that happened to me I'd have nightmares for a month."

"I thought you're not afraid of anything," I teased.

"Yeah, but corpses are really creepy."

We stood like that, holding hands, neither one of us speaking.

"Anyway, I'm alive," she said in a husky voice. She stepped so close to me, the tip of her nose brushed the tip of mine.

There's a little cushion of space that surrounds and moves with us wherever we are. I never realized that, until Jazzy stepped into my space as if she owned it, as if she had been just waiting for the moment when she could slip inside. We kissed. It was an amazingly long kiss, and I tasted salt on the inside of her mouth.

CiTY OF niGHT

THE NEXT MORNING Dan and I loaded our gear onto the *Morrison Hotel* and backed out of the slip. I started to move to the front of the boat, but Dan motioned me to join him in the cabin. When I sat beside him, he passed me a plastic box.

"You wanna pick some new music this morning?" he asked. The box contained about a dozen eight-track cassettes: the Doors, some Beatles, the Rolling Stones, Deep Purple, Cream.

"Can't break tradition," I said, handing him the Doors.

"Damn right," Dan agreed. A moment later the throbbing beat of "Roadhouse Blues" cut through the morning air. You could see it was going to be a beautiful morning, with no trace of yesterday's fog. Dan reached for the throttle and pushed it forward one notch. He took a long sip from an oversized Green Bay Packers coffee mug.

"I got a call from the police last night," Dan said. "They located Raymond Grillo's boat a half mile from where we found the body. They did an autopsy. Turns out he was a single guy—a stockbroker—and he'd mixed vodka with Quaaludes. That's a very bad combination, a death wish if I've ever heard one. He must've been completely stoned when he decided to take a ride on his boat. Guy fell overboard and drowned."

"Wow." It was the only thing I could think of to say.

"I saw my first dead person in 1968 when I was in Vietnam." He took a deep breath. "That's one memory I could do without. Anyway, I promise you today will be boring, like usual."

"Good," I said.

As the day continued, I noticed Dan acting differently toward me, almost friendly. For the first time he actually brought up various topics to talk about: the weather, insurance for his boat, other clammers on the bay. Although I was glad for the change, I wasn't feeling very talkative. I wanted to wrap myself in silence. I wanted to let my body automatically do its thing, working the heavy tongs open and shut, up and down, so I could think about Jazzy.

Around eleven I finally got a long stretch of quiet. I couldn't hide from the fact that the girl I'd been with last night was my first cousin. I had a list of excuses in my head.

1. It only happened because of yesterday's bizarre corpse incident.
2. People often get loony when there's a full moon.
3. I wasn't myself last night. I'd been body-snatched, pure and simple.
4. It was a once-in-a-lifetime experience. It would never happen again.

That's what I tried to tell myself, and I tried hard, but I've never been very good at telling myself a lie and believing it was true. The temperature rose through the morning, and as I worked up a heavy sweat my head got clearer and clearer. Last night, I realized, I hadn't been the least bit body-snatched. Last night I knew exactly what I was doing.

"You look trashed," Dan said while we finished our lunch.

"I am." I had the urge to take a long nap, like yesterday.

"You need an energy boost." He handed me a bar of chocolate.

"Thanks." Bert watched me unwrap the chocolate. He had totally ignored the lettuce and carrots Dan had thrown to him but now jumped all over the chocolate morsel I tossed his way. Bert the junk-food seagull.

"I was a little harsh the other day when your friend

showed up to come clamming," Dan said. "If he still wants to come, bring him along."

"Really?"

"Just make sure he understands we've got to put in a full day's work."

I finished the chocolate and lowered the clam tongs into the water. Dan turned on the Doors, Jim Morrison singing, "City of night . . ." Two weeks ago the word *night* only meant not working to me, a time when I could collapse into bed. My baked, battered body wanted nothing more than that. I never wore a watch, never cared about time. Jazzy had changed everything. Now I began rooting for the hours to speed by. I kept looking south, searching for the ruffled water that would signal the One O'Clock Chop. There would be only a few more hours of work after that.

That night, Jazzy and I stole off together. Mom was working extra hours at the hospital, so she went to sleep by ten. Jazzy and I waited a half hour before we sneaked out of the house and headed for the woods.

"What'd you do all day?" I asked when we were far from the house.

"Not too much," she said quietly. "Thought about stuff."

"What kind of stuff?" I asked, but didn't wait for her

answer. I stopped. In one fluid motion she turned in to my arms and I pulled her against me. Our knees pushed together. I slid my right hand under her black hair, which smelled sweet-clean against my face. She slowly ran her hands down my back—I felt her fingers grab the back belt loops of my jeans. My mouth found hers.

"No," she said.

All day I'd been thinking about kissing her, so now that one word sent an icy jolt through my chest. "What?"

"Don't smile," she said. "I can't kiss you if your mouth is all tight like that. You've got to make your lips relax."

"Like this?" I tried again. This time she kissed back, parting her lips. I felt her hand caressing my neck.

"Yeah, boy," she whispered. "Now, that's my kine kiss, soft and slow."

"Huh?"

"Oops, sorry, I'm speaking pidgin again. *Kine* means kind of."

"Do you mind this?" I asked. "I mean, you know, us."

"Kissin' cousins?" Her throat made a soft, laughing sound.

"You think it's . . . wrong?" I asked.

"No. You?"

"No."

Now I had two Jazzys: the girl staying at our house, and the one I knew when we were alone together. I had to remember to keep the two of them apart when it came to Mom.

Over the next few days we went for walks, on bike rides, to the movies. I took Jazzy to Hunt's Marina so she could look at the Boston Whaler I was saving up for. But our favorite spot was the hideaway in the woods. We went there whenever we got the chance.

It sort of became our thing, her licking the salt lick before kissing me, and the salty taste of her in my mouth. Salt was one of our secrets. One night Mom took us to the La Grange Inn, a real nice restaurant, for dinner. Jazzy and I both ordered the T-bone steak specials. Mom got blackened flounder, her favorite.

"This steak is great," I said, cutting a big juicy piece.

"How's yours?" Mom asked Jazzy.

"De-lish," Jazzy agreed. "Hey, Matt, you want some salt?" Her dark eyes glittered as she slid the salt shaker to my side of the table.

After we all watched *Hawaii Five-O* that evening, Mom said goodnight. It was pouring rain outside, so Jazzy and I stayed in the den and talked. I'd never been that good at chatting with girls, but it felt easy with Jazzy. She told me about school, her friends, a local restaurant called Chunky's that served the best burgers in Hawaii. I talked to her about Trevor, Dan, Mom, and Dad.

"Do you see your dad much?" she asked.

"I usually visit in the summer, and for Thanksgiving or Christmas."

"Is he rich?"

"Yeah, maybe. He's building a new house, a big one, so he's got some bucks. Sometimes he sends me expensive presents. Last year he gave me this great bike and it wasn't even my birthday, or Christmas."

"A Disney Daddy," Jazzy said.

"Huh?"

"A Disney Daddy is a divorced father who spends lots of money on his kids instead of spending time with them."

"That sounds . . . harsh," I said. "He's not that bad. He's always trying to get me to visit him in Montana."

"Come visit me in Hawaii."

It made me happy to see the pleading look on her face. "Why would I want to go to an ugly place like that?"

Reaching over, she smacked me on the arm. Then, in a whisper, she asked, "Are you as close to your dad as you are to your mom?"

"No."

"But you miss him, huh?"

"Yeah. A lot."

"We've got that in common," Jazzy said. "I miss my daddy, too."

One night at the salt lick the mosquitoes dive-bombed us, so I got some mosquito netting and hung it from two bushes. I brought my small lantern. Jazzy talked to me from inside the netting.

"Knock, knock," I said. "Can I come in?"

"Not until you speak the magic word."

"Little pig, little pig, let me in," I said. "Seriously. These bugs are drinking my blood."

"That's because you're so sweet. Say the magic word."

"Fried dough."

"That's two words," she pointed out.

"Okay. Jazz."

"Nope," she said. "Try again."

"Jazzy—"

"The magic word is *question*," she told me. "Go ahead, ask me a question. Anything. Don't think, just ask."

"What do you like about me?" I blurted out.

"Who says I like you?" She laughed. "Well, yeah, I do like you. A lot. You're sweet and strong. You're real nice to your mom. Plus, you're cute. Cute nose and cute earlobes. You're a year younger than me. And we live over five thousand miles apart. And you're my first cousin. But besides that . . ."

I laughed. "Well, you're real nice, too."

"Yeah?" Pause. "Maybe I'm not as nice as you think."

We tried to kiss through the gauzy cloth. It made my mouth tickle.

She pulled me inside the netting.

MONEY IN THE BANK

I ARRIVED AT THE DOCK at five minutes before seven; Trevor showed up a few minutes later. He was dressed in a gray plaid flannel shirt with rubber overalls that tucked into thigh-high rubber boots. He looked like he'd just stepped out of an L. L. Bean catalogue. When Dan saw him, he scowled for a moment but then burst out laughing.

"You look like a duck hunter! You're going to broil in all that rubber stuff! I hope you got shorts and a T-shirt underneath."

"I do." Trevor smiled weakly. "Look, I promise I won't be any trouble. You won't even notice I'm on your boat."

"Oh, really?" Dan studied Trevor closely. "You got water? You bring a lunch?"

"Yep. My mom made a batch of double-fudge brownies."

"With or without nuts?" Dan demanded.

"With," Trevor said carefully.

"Well, in that case you can come on board."

Trevor sneaked me a smile as he walked past. A few minutes later Dan backed the *Morrison Hotel* out of the slip and nosed it down the canal, heading for the bay. Trevor sat next to me at the bow, briskly rubbing his hands together.

"So. Are clams solitary hunters, like sharks? Or do they swim in schools?"

"If you start acting stupid," I warned, "Dan will eat you for lunch."

Suddenly the music started blaring.

"The Doors!" Trevor jerked his head around to look at Dan. "Jim Morrison! That guy was a genius."

Dan nodded at me. "Your friend's got good taste."

We anchored just east of the Robert Moses Causeway. Trevor stood back and watched us get ready to work.

"Where did you put the dead guy?" Trevor asked.

"Right here," Dan said, pointing at the deck. "Maybe *you'll* get lucky and pull one up today."

"I'd rather not," Trevor said. "But I do want to try clamming."

"Knock yourself out." Dan handed him my tongs. It was funny seeing Trevor awkwardly maneuvering the tongs in the water, but he did get three clams on his first pull.

"Not bad!" Dan winked at me. "The mother lode!"

After Trevor dug a few dozen clams he grew bored, and I took over. The day got hot. Trevor peeled off his flannel shirt and rubber overalls. There was a faint offshore breeze, and it carried the strong smell of fresh-brewed coffee. Just another day on the Great South Bay—me busting my butt while someone on land enjoyed a leisurely breakfast.

"How're you doing?" Dan asked from his side of the boat.

"I'm not getting squat," I said, slapping at my thigh. Horseflies were making my life miserable.

Dan dunked a rag in cold water and tied it around his head. He went back to the cabin and turned up the music again.

"Are you going to move to another spot?" Trevor asked.

"Nope." Dan shook his head. "On a day like today you just have to dig deeper. I'm not going in 'til I've got two bushels, at least."

The morning dragged on. Trevor talked nonstop about summer school, Allison, a bad horror movie he'd just seen, and the Vega GT Coupe he had his eye on.

"Shh!" I finally told him. "I gotta concentrate."

On Jazzy. Thinking of her was better than a long drink of ice water, but Trevor's chitchat made it hard to focus.

At noon the three of us sat down for lunch. Bert arrived a minute later, jutting out his beak, moving briskly about the boat.

"He walks around like he owns the place!" Trevor exclaimed.

"Bert is the boss around here," Dan agreed. "He shows up to make sure we're doing our jobs."

"He seems pretty cool," Trevor observed.

"I've only seen him get mad once," Dan said. "That was last year, when another seagull tried to muscle in on his territory."

"What happened?"

"It was like a heavyweight fight. You should've seen it. Feathers all over the place. Bert finally fought him off."

"Do you clam all year 'round?" Trevor asked.

"Nah, bay is usually frozen by January. I work 'til late November, and then I pick up some part-time work as a janitor for a few months. I start clamming again in March."

"Must be freezing out here in January," I said.

"Brutal." Dan took out a pocketknife and began slicing open a pomegranate. "When the One O'Clock Chop hits, it goes right through you, I don't care how many layers you're wearing."

"What about the cove?" Trevor asked.

Dan shot him a look. Then he looked over at me, suspicious.

"What is it with you guys and the cove?"

"I've heard so many rumors about that place," Trevor said.

"I wouldn't know, because I don't clam there, period." Dan spat seeds over the side. "I've heard all the stories—clams so thick you can make two bushels in less than an hour, if you don't get caught. But I've got no respect for that. If just one person gets sick from bad clams it'll be all over the TV news and the authorities will shut down this bay. Clamming is how I make my living. If they close down the bay, who's going to pay my bills, huh? Who's going to pay my mortgage?"

As we were driving back, I spotted Jazzy waiting at the far end of the dock. We all waved to her.

Dan looked at me. "You know, your cousin's not the ugliest girl I've ever seen."

"If she wasn't related to you," Trevor pointed out, "you'd have it made in the shade."

"Yeah," I agreed nonchalantly.

"I was thinking maybe we could hook up," Trevor said.

"Jazzy and . . . you?"

"Why not?"

"What about Allison?" I asked.

"She's history. I'm breaking up with her. So what do you think?"

Dan cut the engine and we sat in the water just outside the dock. All the slips were taken, and we had to wait for one to open up.

"About what?" I was stalling, trying to think of something to say.

"Me and Jazzy. Think she might go for it?"

I shrugged. "Jazzy does things her own way. She's hard to predict."

Trevor waved again at Jazzy. "You could put in a good word for me."

"I could." But I knew who Jazzy was smiling at.

When I came home that afternoon I added thirty-six dollars to the other bills crammed in my shoe box. I was almost halfway to being able to buy the Boston Whaler.

I got out of the shower and checked myself in the mirror. My skin was darkly tanned, and my hair had been lightened by the sun. My body wasn't ripped like Dan's, probably never would be. But three solid weeks of clamming had added some new definition to my shoulders, arms, biceps, and pecs. That was money in the bank, too.

But it was Jazzy who made me feel rich.

At night we huddled together under the mosquito netting. She made a soft humming sound whenever we kissed. Tonight while we were kissing she took my hands and moved them up to her chest. I wasn't ready for that; a few seconds later I moved my hands away.

"What?" she whispered.

"I don't know."

She pulled back and looked at me.

"Feels funny." That sounded lame, so I tried to explain. "Not you. *I* feel funny, I guess."

"It's okay if I want you to," she pointed out.

"I know." I didn't sound convinced because I wasn't.

"It's okay, really, I'm glad." I knew she was trying to reassure me. "At least you're not always trying to grab me like other guys I've gone out with."

I said nothing. She really didn't sound so glad.

"The thing is, it's all *me*," she said softly. "Do you believe in God?"

"Huh?" At that particular moment "God" was the very last word I expected her to say.

"Do you believe in God?"

"Yeah."

"Aha!" She sounded triumphant. "You *do* believe in God!"

"Yes."

"Do you believe that, A, God is up in heaven? Or do you believe that, B, God is everywhere?"

"I'll choose B," I replied. "Everywhere."

"I believe that, too! God is everywhere—in my hair, my eyes, my brain, my lips. But God's here, too." She touched her breast. "I know he is."

I had no answer to that. It seemed like an airtight argument, but she didn't move my hands back to her chest. So that was the end of that. And, to be honest, I didn't know whether to feel disappointed or relieved.

July 31

RED SKY IN THE MORNING

EVERY DAY OF WORK meant more good stuff coming my way: money, muscle, and toughness. But every hour clamming also meant one more hour away from Jazzy.

I bought a watch, hoping it might somehow hurry the workday along. I bought a calendar, too, so I could keep track of the days Jazzy and I still had left.

August 28 was when Jazzy'd fly back to Hawaii. Whenever I thought of that day, I got a feeling of dread. Time on Dan's boat took forever to pass, but it seemed like August 28 was rocketing toward us.

At the beginning of the summer, when Mom and I left for work, Jazzy had kept herself busy reading, listening to music, or playing guitar. It didn't take long for her to get bored of that routine, though. Mom mentioned the animal shelter near the hospital where she worked. Jazzy was wild about dogs and cats. They didn't have any paid jobs, but she happily signed up as a volunteer. Mom's nursing schedule had changed to the early shift, so now they both got up when I did, and Mom dropped Jazzy off on the way to work.

That morning, Jazzy took Mom's bike and rode with me to the dock. There was an eerie glow in the sky. As we rode, Jazzy chattered on about her new job at the shelter, which she seemed to like.

"It's crazy loud in there—lots of barking and meowing. And sometimes it's kind of sad. Yesterday they brought in this adorable cocker spaniel someone found on the street— no tags, nothing. Abandoned. Hey." She jumped off her bike. "What kind of flowers are these?"

"Honeysuckle. That's one of Mom's favorite words."

"Honeysuckle." Jazzy pulled off three blossoms and put them in her hair. "My favorite Hawaiian word is *humuhumunukunukuapua'a*."

I stared at her. "You gotta be kidding!"

"For real," she said, laughing.

"Say it again!"

"*Humuhumunukunukuapua'a*." She grinned. "Twenty-one letters. It's a kind of Hawaiian fish. If you can spell the word right, you get a special prize. I'll give it to you myself tonight."

We quickly kissed. Then she squeezed me in a hug.

When we reached the docks, Dan waved from the *Morrison Hotel*.

"Mor-ning," Jazzy said in a singsong voice. "Beautiful day, huh?"

The sky was stained blood red; the same color was mirrored in the canal.

"Could be trouble brewing," Dan said, lifting the clam tongs onto the boat. "You know what they say. 'Red sky at night, sailor's delight. Red sky in morning, sailor's warning.'"

"Did you hear anything on the marine radio?" I asked.

"Nah. Just some rain, but it should hold off until later tonight." Dan turned on a slow Doors song: "Riders on the Storm." I untied the lines on the bow and stern. Jazzy waved from the dock as we moved down the canal.

By now I'd been clamming for about a month, and I didn't feel like a rookie anymore. I worked hard, but I knew how to pace myself so I didn't poop out by mid-morning like I did the first few weeks.

"Have you ever been married?" I asked Dan later in the morning.

"Yeah, I was married for two years. A good-looking woman, too, but she ran off with some pencil-neck geek who had a flashy smile and a load of money." He spat over the side.

"That's too bad." I felt sorry I'd brought it up.

He shrugged. "She ran off with him five years ago. As a matter of fact, the anniversary is Wednesday of next week. That night I intend to set up a command post at Codfish Bob's and drink about half a bottle of good Irish whiskey. It's a personal tradition of mine. I'm thinking we just might get a late start Thursday morning. You don't mind, do you?"

"Okay by me." I smiled.

"Since we're playing Twenty Questions," Dan said, "I've got one for you. Why do you keep letting Frank short you at the clam scale?"

"I don't."

"Oh, really. How much did he pay you for your clams yesterday? Thirty-six bucks?"

"I think so, yeah."

"But you really earned thirty-eight."

"Two bucks," I said. "Whoop-dee-doo."

"Yeah, but it's *your* two bucks," Dan said.

I shrugged. "It doesn't matter that much to me."

Dan shook his head. "That little weasel has been doing that to you all summer. Two bucks here, dollar and a half there. Don't seem like much, but it adds up. He wouldn't dare try that with me, but he figures with a kid he can get away with it. There are plenty of Franks in the world, folks who are more than happy to take two dollars, five dollars, a hundred dollars out of your wallet. Until you stop them. I was going to talk to him. But I realized it's your fight, not mine."

"It's really not a big deal, Dan." I appreciated his concern, but mostly I wanted to stop talking. I had better things to think about.

"How'd you do today?" Mom asked when I came home.

"Not so great." I flopped into a chair by the kitchen table.

"What's wrong?"

"I got a blister in the afternoon." I showed her my right thumb. I could feel my sweat-soaked T-shirt clinging to the back of the chair. "I couldn't really use my hand after that, so I was pretty worthless. Where's Jazzy?"

She put a finger to her mouth. "Sleeping."

I went to my room. In my notebook I recorded the date, weight of the clams I'd dug (thirty-three pounds), and how much I'd earned (nineteen dollars). From my bottom drawer I removed the box, dumped out the money, and counted it up. Even after today's poor haul, I still had a grand total of four hundred and forty-seven dollars. Not bad at all. In the kitchen Mom handed me a glass of lemonade with lots of ice. I tried to hold it up to my forehead, but I had too much hair.

"You want me to put something on that blister?" she asked.

"In a sec," I said. "Can you give me a haircut first?"

"Right now?" she asked. "All right, come on."

I followed her outside to the porch. Mom got the electric clippers and plugged them into the outside socket. She'd been cutting my hair since I can remember—she was the only barber I'd ever had. I felt her move the clippers behind my left ear, sending buzzing vibrations deep into my skull.

"Jazzy and I had lunch together at the hospital cafeteria," she said. "We had a long talk today about my brother Neal. It brought up lots of memories."

"Happy or sad?"

"Well, both. I really miss him, you know? Having her here almost feels like being with my brother." She turned off the clippers and changed attachments. "How close do you want me to cut it?"

"Medium-short."

"You sure? Most boys wear their hair long nowadays."

"I don't care. I just want to be cool when I'm working."

"Okay. I ran into Jazzy's boss at the animal shelter—he said she's doing a great job. She's wonderful, don't you think?"

"Kinda nice," I agreed, trying to sound casual.

"Just nice?" Mom laughed. "Hold still. Look down at your heart."

I dropped my chin onto my chest. Mom said that whenever she cut my hair: *"Look down at your heart."* When I was little I thought my mother knew just about everything, so it was no stretch to believe that she really could see into my heart. What would she say if she could see into my heart now?

"There you go, young man." She held out her hand. "That'll be five dollars."

I smiled. "Could I pay you next time?"

"Oh, I suppose . . ." She flicked some clumps of hair off my shoulder. "Hey, that's one heckuva haircut."

"I feel cooler already."

"She sure is pretty," Mom said.

"Huh?"

She stared at me. "Jazzy."

"I guess so." I shrugged. "I'm going to go shower off this hair."

"Okay. I'll find something for that blister."

FIREWORKS

I GOT HOME FROM WORK at four thirty. Jazzy and Mom were in the kitchen, working on the crossword.

"'Flabbergasted,'" Mom said. "Seven letters."

"'Amazed'?" Jazzy suggested.

"'Shocked,'" Mom said and wrote down the word.

"Hi, guys."

Jazzy looked up and grinned. "Hi, Matt."

Mom pointed at the counter. "There's a package from your father."

When I unwrapped it I found a bunch of business cards.

MATTHEW CARTER
Bivalve Extractor

I showed them to Mom.

"Your father always did have a good sense of humor," Mom said. I couldn't tell whether she was being sincere or sarcastic.

"Hey, I'm making pork chops for supper," Jazzy told me.

"Wish I didn't have this headache."

Mom gave me a sympathetic look. "Take some aspirin and lie down. We won't eat for another hour. Jazzy, let's do one more. 'Antonym for *hates*.'"

"That's the opposite, huh? 'Likes'? 'Loves'?"

Mom shook her head. "Has to be six letters."

"'Adores'?" Jazzy lifted her brown eyes and gave me a secret smile.

I took Mom's advice and lay down for a half hour. At supper, Jazzy told us about her work at the animal shelter.

"We've got a boa constrictor—Brenda. She's enormous. Must weigh fifty pounds. My thigh is as thick as her middle."

"Good heavens!" Mom said.

"People buy pets like boas and alligators when they're small and cute," Jazzy explained. "When they grow big, their owners don't want them anymore, which is so unfair. I feel sorry for Brenda. I always go over and talk to her, make sure she's okay. She's sweet."

Mom gave me a pointed look. "Don't even think about it, Matt!"

"I won't, I won't," I told her.

If any other girl I knew worked at an animal shelter, I guarantee she would have been gaga over some cute kitten or dog. For Jazzy it was a boa constrictor. No wonder I was crazy about her.

I had promised to take Jazzy to a dance at the Babylon Yacht Club that night. There would be a rock band, dancing, fireworks, the whole shebang, and I was really looking forward to it. I had hoped the aspirin would knock out my pounding headache, but it didn't. There was no way I could go.

"I'm really sorry," I told Jazzy after dinner.

"That's too bad," she told me. "Alice offered to take me. I think I might go for an hour or so."

"Have fun," I said.

I went to bed. A little later the phone woke me from a deep sleep. It was Trevor.

"What's up?" he asked. "You chillin' like a villain?"

"I *was* sleeping."

"Why aren't you at the dance?" he asked.

"Headache." But I realized my headache was now gone. And it wasn't even nine thirty. "I feel better. But I don't have a ride."

"My uncle's going to drive me," Trevor said. "We'll pick you up. Be ready in ten minutes."

I got dressed in my white high-top Chuck Taylor Converse sneakers, brown corduroy pants, and my favorite Hershey's T-shirt, faded but clean. Mom's bedroom door was closed; the house was quiet. I left a note for Mom and went outside to wait for Trevor. After that long nap my head felt water-logged. For some reason Jazzy's Hawaiian word, *humuhu-munukunukuapua'a*, kept swimming through my mind. When Trevor picked me up, I pulled one of the Bivalve Extractor business cards Dad had sent me from my back pocket and handed it to him.

"Cool!" Trevor grinned. "I wish my dad had a twisted sense of humor!"

The Babylon Yacht Club was packed. As we entered, I noticed all the couples, kids walking with their arms around each other. It gave me a sad feeling to realize that, as first cousins, Jazzy and I would never be able to walk like that. What we had would have to stay private.

"Guys!"

Trevor and I turned and saw Trevor's ex-girlfriend, Allison.

"Hey, kiddo," Trevor said.

"Hey." She didn't smile at him.

"Allison, have you seen Jazzy?" I asked.

She shook her head but in a nervous way, like maybe she wasn't telling the truth. I started walking toward the music.

The band was playing "Whole Lotta Love" by Led Zeppelin when I walked onto the dance floor. Then I saw her. Them.

Jazzy and Tommy O'Rourke. They didn't see me. She was dressed in the outfit she wore the first time I laid eyes on her. Tommy was wearing a black T-shirt "accidentally" ripped halfway up. They were slow dancing. She was smiling into his eyes, arms around him, her thumbs hooked through the back loops of his jeans.

I couldn't breathe.

I started running and could hear Trevor behind me. "Wait! Where you going, Matt? They haven't done the fireworks yet!"

But I'd seen enough. Zigzagging through the crowd, I made my way back to the entrance of the yacht club, and then I was gone.

DREAM OF THE
LAND CLAMS

HAVE YOU EVER had the wind knocked out of you? It doesn't sound serious, but it's the most terrifying feeling in the world. I fell out of a tree when I was about seven, and I couldn't speak because I couldn't breathe. I was sure I was going to die.

I felt that way now—like all the breath, and blood, had been sucked out of me. There are no words to accurately describe how empty, how hollow, how voidal (if that's even a word) I felt seeing Jazzy tangled up with Tommy O'Rourke.

It was unusually dark that night. There was no moon, and so I had to walk blindly, using my feet to feel the edge of the road. The rain started just as I crawled into bed. I hated myself for waking up and going to the dance. Bad move, Matt. Somebody should invent a machine that lets you insert your life like a tape and press REWIND. Or ERASE. I wanted to pull a Rip Van

Winkle and go to bed for twenty years, but I couldn't sleep. I lay there, wide awake, listening for Jazzy's return, and cursing myself for doing it. My imagination went wild picturing them together—talking, kissing, Tommy touching her . . . there. I could see every detail with perfect clarity.

In sixth grade I wrote a school report about the Aztecs. In the 1400s and 1500s they built a great civilization. But, man, were they bloodthirsty! When it came to human sacrifice, the Aztecs won hands down. Some Aztec warriors would slit open an enemy's chest, then cut out his heart and show it to him. So his own heart was the last thing he saw before he died.

Dear Jazzy: You ripped my heart out of my chest and showed it to me at the very moment the us *of us died.*

How's that for self-pity?

I couldn't sleep, so I got out of bed. Turning on the light, I spotted the business cards Dad had sent me. I carried the cards to the kitchen and stuffed them in the trash.

Finally, at twelve twenty-one, I heard the sound of the front door opening. It wasn't until I heard Jazzy shut her bedroom door that I let myself close my eyes. Even then I was absolutely sure I could hear her heart beating in her room, until I finally realized that the sound I heard was my own.

A dream. I was walking up the path to the front of our house. It was sunset. Mom and Dad were there, married like before. I heard a hissing sound from under the bushes. When I walked over to look, I saw something spit. At first I figured it must be some kind of frog, but when I knelt down I saw them—clams! There were thousands of them. And they were alive.

"Dad!" I yelled. "C'mere! Land clams!"

He smiled and waved, and I wasn't sure that he believed me, but I didn't even care. It was a miracle—a bed of clams in Mom's flower bed!

When I woke at five thirty, I could still imagine those land clams. But it's a cruel thing to wake and realize that what made you feel good was only a dream.

August 3

UNSALTED

In the morning I found a note slipped under my door.

> *Dear Matt,*
> *Allison said you came to the dance and saw me and*
> *left, mad. I want to explain, but there's not really*
> *much to say. It just kind of happened.*
> *I feel awful if I hurt you.*
> *You've been so incredibly sweet.*
>
> > *Feeling sad (and guilty),*
> > *Jazzy*

I folded the note, dressed without taking a shower, ate a quick bowl of cereal, and made my lunch. Ten after six. I was glad nobody was awake yet. I rummaged through the junk drawer until I found a pack of matches. Then I eased open the back door and climbed onto my bike. When I reached the honeysuckle bush I stopped, unfolded the note, and read it again.

I feel awful if I hurt you.

If?

I struck a match. I lit Jazzy's note on fire. Within seconds, all the words had turned to ash.

And then it was just another morning: Dan and me riding out to the bay while the demonic voice of Jim Morrison blared out over the engine's roar. Dan stood watching me set the anchor.

"You look terrible," he told me.

"That's what you said yesterday."

"Yeah, well, it's even truer today." He lifted down the tongs and handed them to me. "You been burnin' the candle, huh?"

"I guess so," I admitted.

"Maybe I should give you The Talk. You know, The Talk a father has with his son the first time he has a real girlfriend."

"You don't need to," I told him.

"I don't?"

"Nope." I let my tongs splash into the water. "I broke up with someone last night. Or she broke up with me."

"Yeah? How come?"

"Guess she found someone she likes better." It hurt to say that, but in a strange way the hurt felt good.

Dan nodded. "That's too bad, kid."

I didn't say much after that. Instead I tried to concentrate on digging clams, slow and steady, falling into the rhythm my body knew by heart. Lower the tongs, work them shut, lift, shake, haul up, spill out, lower the tongs . . . It was mindless, boring work—perfect for the mood I was in—and by now I could practically do it in my sleep. I figured the harder I worked, the less time I'd have to think. The tongs got heavier and heavier as the day wore on, but I continued working hard, almost enjoying the scream of my muscles. By four o'clock I'd dug a bushel and a peck. Dan ended with three bushels and a half. Bert feasted on our throwaways. A good day all around, considering. The sacks of clams made an impressive mound on the front of our boat as we headed in.

Right then we saw a white boat speeding in our direction. It seemed to come out of nowhere, and it was flat-out flying, heading toward us on a collision course.

"HEY!" Dan screamed. "WATCH WHERE YOU'RE GOING!"

The white boat stubbornly refused to change his course.

"WHAT ARE YOU DOING?" Dan screamed. Now the boat was close enough so we could see two guys, big and tanned, maybe college kids. Dan maintained his speed, still believing they would slow down, but they didn't. At the last moment Dan swore, cut our engine, and swerved to the right. The two guys waved, laughing, as their boat crossed barely ten feet in front of us. I let out a breath.

"That was close!" I said.

"WATCH OUT!" Dan screamed, pointing at the wake made by the other boat. The *Morrison Hotel* rode low in the water, especially when it was loaded with clams. We hit their wake, hard. Our boat bounced up, the deck tilting at a steep angle.

"THE CLAMS!" Dan screamed. The burlap sacks were piled against the cabin in the middle of the boat. I scrambled back from the bow, trying to stay low on the twisting, slippery deck, but before I could get there one of Dan's bushels fell onto its side. I grabbed it, but not before a bunch of clams spilled overboard.

"Sorry, Dan, I—"

"Not your fault." He was furious, but his voice stayed calm. "How much did I lose?"

"At least a peck," I guessed.

Dan grabbed the bushel from me and lifted it. "More like a third."

"Do you know those guys?" I asked.

"Not yet, but I will," Dan said grimly.

We continued heading in, but we didn't go back to the regular dock. Instead we cruised two auxiliary docks farther west. Dan used binoculars to search the shore.

"Bingo," he said, pointing at a small dock at the end of a canal. He handed me his binoculars. It was them, all right, and the two guys were still on the white boat. Dan brought us in at a fast clip, ignoring the DEAD SLOW sign. When we got close he gunned the engine in reverse to slow us down and then killed it. The *Morrison Hotel* drifted straight toward them. The two guys looked up, startled, as Dan jumped onto their boat.

"What the—"

"SHUT UP!" Dan bellowed, grabbing the guy's shirt. The guy looked scared. "You wanna tell me which one of you pretty boys was driving when you decided to play chicken out there?"

They just looked at each other.

"I was," the other one admitted.

Dan let go of the one guy and approached the other. "You think it's funny cutting people off like that?"

"Sorry," he said meekly.

"When I hit your wake, I lost some clams. A third of a bushel of *my* clams, culled and washed, lying on the bottom of this bay."

"Sorry," the guy said again, which sounded pretty lame. He stood there, waiting, and I almost felt bad for him.

"'Sorry' won't put my clams back onto my boat," Dan told him. "Your screwing around just cost you twenty-five bucks."

The guy immediately removed a twenty and a five from his wallet. It was obvious that more than anything they wanted Dan to go away.

"We were just goofing," the other guy said. "We didn't mean nothing."

"If you ever try to wake me like that again," Dan said evenly, "I promise I'll pull you off your boat and coldcock you. Is there any part of that you don't understand?"

They shook their heads no.

"Good." Dan turned around. Without another word, he started our engine and we backed away.

Coldcock. I loved the sound of that word. I was almost disappointed that Dan hadn't hit him right there and then.

After I sold my clams I spotted Trevor waiting beside the bike rack. He handed me a can of Coke, which felt unbelievably cold when I pressed it against my forehead. I told him about what happened with Dan and the two college guys.

"I've never seen anybody that mad," I said.

"Oh yeah?" Trevor smiled. "You looked pretty mad last night . . ."

He let the sentence trail off, dangling like a juicy worm before a hungry fish.

"Was it because of seeing Jazzy with Tommy?" he asked.

Instead of answering I took a long drink of soda.

"I was thinking it didn't make a lot of sense," Trevor said, "you getting all pissed off like that, if she's just your cousin."

This time I met Trevor's look, head-on. I finished the Coke and crumpled the can. When I stuffed the wreckage into my backpack, I realized that Trevor knew the truth.

"Oh," he mumbled. "Sorry. I didn't know. . . ."

"Yeah, well, now you do."

We walked away from the dock, and for once Trevor knew enough to keep his mouth shut.

I didn't want to go home that afternoon, but I had no choice. Entering the back door, I realized I was walking silently, like a burglar in my own house. Jazzy's bedroom door was closed, but I could hear her playing the guitar and singing:

Momma standin' in the kitchen
cookin' stew and sticky rice

I stood listening outside her bedroom, eyes closed, leaning my head against the doorjamb. I wanted to walk away, but her voice held me fast.

Daddy's talkin' story
with his friends all night

I couldn't move. Why couldn't she sing off-key and croaky?

Mom came home from work an hour later. She didn't feel like cooking, so we went out to the Pioneer Diner. Jazzy sat in a booth across from me. She looked beautiful in a thin pink sweater, with a matching bow in her hair. She was wearing her puka-shell necklace, too. Up until then I'd been able to avoid facing her one on one, but when Mom went to the restroom, there was no place to hide.

"I feel awful," she began.

"I bet."

"I do!" she protested.

We fell silent. What was the point of talking about it? What could either one of us say? Jazzy looked like she was about to cry. The waitress saved the day by bringing our salads. I occupied myself by trying to spear cherry tomatoes with my fork until Mom came back to the table. She pointed at Jazzy's untouched salad.

"Not hungry?"

"Guess I'm not in the mood for salad," Jazzy answered in a small voice.

"Jazzy met a boy at the dance." Mom was talking to me. "He's asked her to go to the movies tonight. His name is Tommy O'Rourke. Do you know him?"

In my head I pictured Tommy O'Rourke. Tonight he'd be sitting with Jazzy—my Jazzy—in a dark movie theater.

He's a punk, Mom, I wanted to say. *He's been breaking the law, digging clams in the cove to pay for his new boat. He's a major-league slimeball.* I opened my mouth, but those words wouldn't come out. I shrugged, like I was bored and couldn't care less.

"It's none of my business," I finally said.

"Do you know him?" Mom pressed me.

"I know who he is. He's not an axe murderer or anything."

Mom laughed. "I'm glad to hear that! I don't mean to pry, Jazzy, but I think your mother would want me to be aware of what you're doing. What time will you be home?"

"Eleven thirty?"

"I'd be more comfortable if you're in by eleven," Mom told her.

Jazzy nodded. "Sure."

The waitress brought our dinner. Automatically, the way I always did, I reached for the salt. But I sensed that Jazzy was watching me. It had been our private joke, but all that felt like ancient history. With a great effort I pulled back my hand, leaving the salt shaker untouched at the edge of the table.

DEMOLITION DERBY

DAN TAUGHT ME THINGS. He explained how to read the buoys when passing through the mouth of the bay. For instance, "red right return" meant that you had to keep the red buoy on your right when you returned to the dock in the harbor. He showed me how to double-anchor the boat to stabilize it when the bay got extra choppy. He taught me how to tie a square knot, sailor's knot, bowline, and half-hitch. One afternoon, while we were taking a break, he taught me how to throw a punch.

"You ever been in a fistfight?"

"Not really," I admitted.

"I'm not recommending violence," he said. "But if you need to hit a guy, you'd better know what you're doing if you don't wanna get your ass handed to you on a silver platter. C'mon. Show me how you'd hit me."

I smiled—Dan Piersall was about the last guy on earth I'd choose to fight. I stood and made a fist with my right hand.

"Stop right there." He pointed at my hand—I'd tucked my thumb into my fist. "If you hit someone like that you'll break your thumb, guaranteed. Try it again."

Weakly, I swung at him. He bobbed out of the way.

"Not bad. Put your fist about six inches in front of your shoulder." He crouched in a boxer's pose. "Don't swing your arm—drive through the punch, like this."

Lightly, he hit me on the shoulder.

"Do you aim for the nose or the mouth?" I asked.

"I'd pop him just above the eye." In slow-motion, he swung his fist and brought it to my right eye. "*Bang!* And don't give him a friendly love tap, either. You want to hit him hard enough so when he goes down, he thinks twice about getting back up."

With all the important stuff Dan taught me, you would have thought that I'd miss my dad less. But the opposite was true. Dan wasn't Dad. I always appreciated it when Dan taught me something, but if anything, it always made me wish I had more Dad in my life.

I knew Dad wouldn't be calling until Friday, but I wanted to speak to him, so Mom let me call him that night. It's not that I had some big issue I needed his help with—I just wanted to hear his voice. At first we talked baseball.

"Did you watch the news?" I asked him. "Phil Niekro just pitched a no-hitter. They showed the last inning on TV."

"I saw that!" Dad exclaimed. "Man, when Niekro's got his knuckleball working, he's vicious. How are the Mets doing?"

"Terrible," I said. "Willie Mays isn't hitting. This is the worst year he's ever had."

"Maybe it's time to hang up his cleats and retire," Dad said. "There comes a time for everyone. But how're you doing, Matt?" Dad asked. "You seem sort of down."

"I've just been working really hard." Then I blurted out: "Dad, do you still go to church?"

"Church?" He sounded surprised. "Well, yeah, Heather and I go once in a while. Why do you ask?"

"Mom still goes three or four times a week, plus Sundays."

"I guess she enjoys it," he said. "Do you go with her?"

"Nope," I told him. "I stopped going to church when you moved out."

That must have been a real conversation stopper, because a moment later he said he had to go.

The next morning Jazzy and Mom huddled together at the kitchen table, working on the crossword.

"'Hawaiian feast,'" Mom said.

"'Luau.'" Jazzy rolled her eyes. "Duhhh!"

"Here's a harder one," Mom said. "'Hawaiian instruments.'"

"'Ukuleles,'" Jazzy replied.

"No, only four letters."

"'Ukes.'" Jazzy grinned.

"I would never have known that!" Mom said. "Pull up a chair, Matt."

But I didn't. I tried my best to act normal so Mom wouldn't notice that anything was wrong. Besides, they had almost finished the puzzle. Maybe I should have been happy to see Mom getting close to Jazzy. But the crossword had always been our special thing.

Mom had taken time off from work so she and Jazzy could go shopping and sightseeing. Two days in a row the house was empty when I came home, which was okay. On Thursday I returned from clamming to find Jazzy sitting in the den watching TV. There was no choice but to play the I'll-avoid-you-if-you-avoid-me dance. Which is what we both did.

The situation couldn't have been worse. Imagine: there's a girl you're crazy about. She breaks up with you, which is bad enough, but she's *living in your house. Sleeping in a bedroom* down the hall. *Going out with another guy, so every day you get to hear her laughing with him on the phone.* It was a nightmare. When Jazzy went out, I couldn't sleep. I'd lie in bed, listening, waiting for her to come home. Feeling jealous was horrible and I hated it, but I couldn't help myself.

One night Jazzy took along her guitar when she went out with Tommy. I imagined her singing to him on a beach, or on his boat. After they left, I walked down to Wheelright Pond. Stripping down to my underwear, I waded into the warm, dark water. I floated on my back, staring up at the Milky Way. It would have been a peaceful way to spend a half hour, if I wasn't so heartsick.

Trevor called a couple of times that week, but I didn't feel like doing anything. Mom and I stayed home and watched TV. After Mom had gone to bed one night, I went outside to revisit the old salt-lick hideaway in the woods. The mosquito netting was still there, hanging limply from the tree. I stuck both arms into the icy springwater and kept them there until I could feel my heart throbbing in my wrists.

My absolute low point came when I tried to use Allison to make Jazzy jealous. Here's my pathetic scheme—phone Allison's house when I knew she would be at work and leave a message asking her to go to the Demolition Derby with me. I'd ask her to call me back during dinnertime, when Jazzy would be home. I wanted Jazzy to see me get the phone call. It was the oldest game in the world, petty and nasty. In other words—perfect. I rehearsed until I knew the exact message I would leave on Allison's answering machine. But when I dialed the number, somebody picked up.

"Hello?" It was Allison.

"Hi, ah, Allison?" I wasn't prepared to actually talk to her. "This is Matt. Matt Carter."

"Hi there!" She seemed glad to hear from me. "What's up, Matt?"

"I thought you might be at work," I said, stalling.

"No, it's my day off." I pictured Barbie-doll Allison. I felt bad about what I was going to do, but I pushed ahead anyway. "Hey, you want to go to the Demolition Derby next Friday?"

"Oh." She sounded disappointed. "Rick Frost asked me last night!"

"Oh, okay. That's cool."

"I'm sorry, Matt. I mean, I'd like to see you. Really. Maybe we could do something another time?"

"Okay, yeah, sure."

Allison began chattering about her annoying younger sister, but I barely listened. I'd just been rejected by a girl I didn't even want to go out with in the first place. Could things get any worse?

"You know, I'm not really into cars," she said.

"What?"

"Cars," she repeated. "At the Demolition Derby."

"Oh, yeah, right. Cars."

Pause. We'd run out of things to say.

"Well, I guess I better go," I said.

"Will you call me another time?" she asked.

"Sure. And hey, when you go to the Demolition Derby, don't sit too close. If you do you'll get oil and mud sprayed all over you. Seriously."

She laughed and thanked me for the advice. I hung up the phone, relieved that my fake date with Allison hadn't worked out after all. I lay down on my bed and closed my eyes.

Maybe it's that simple, I thought. Maybe I just had gotten too close.

August 14

MOTHER LODE

A SMALL SNACK BAR had been set up at the Babylon dock. Dan and I walked over to check it out. There was a homemade sign that said FRESH COFFEE 'N MUFFINS. The girl behind the counter looked familiar. When I got closer I recognized her—Darlene LeClerc, the girl I'd spotted sailing on my first day clamming. She had brown hair pulled back with a blue headband.

"Hey, Darlene."

"Hi, Matt."

"First day of business, huh?" Dan asked.

Darlene nodded. "It's been busy so far. What can I get for you?"

"Coffee, black," Dan said. "You going to be here this afternoon, young lady? I don't suppose you could ice me down a couple of cold beers, could you?"

Darlene grinned. "'Fraid not!" She fixed coffee for Dan and a hot chocolate for me.

"Thanks," I said, handing her a dollar bill.

"Good luck." She flashed me a pretty smile.

As we left the dock I sat up front on the boat, cross-legged, sipping my hot chocolate, watching the bow scissor the glass surface of the bay. Glancing back, I could see Dan's weathered face, the sinews bulging in his neck. I thought of him as a mythic figure, like the Ancient Mariner, or the guy who caught that humongous fish in *The Old Man and the Sea*. Dan was my rock. I loved working with him.

At eleven thirty Dan moved the boat and I set the anchor. Another hot, muggy day; I felt grateful for a bank of clouds running interference on the sun. So far the clamming had been mediocre, at best. My bushel basket was half full, and my energy level lower than that. Mom had made a batch of hermits, loaded with raisins, and I was looking forward to lunch.

My tongs splashed into the water. I worked the handles together until the basket closed, lifted the tongs about one foot, and shook them up and down. It sounded like rocks rumbling around. Hand over hand, I lifted the tongs and spilled them open onto the deck.

Clams. Lots of them.

"Whoa," I said, counting. "Look, Dan. Eighteen. In one load."

"Make sure they're not seed," Dan said. "Sometimes you hit a place where some guy has just finished culling his clams."

I stopped and put the clams into the rack. When I shook the box only one fell through. "They're keepers!"

Dan turned to watch me throw in the tongs. Again, that loud rocky sound. This time twenty-five clams clattered onto the deck. Dan grinned at me slyly.

"Looks like you hit pay dirt. I'm not getting diddly squat over here." He rubbed his forehead with the back of his hand. "I got a proposition for you. I want to move the boat about four feet that way. All right?"

"It's your boat. Why you asking me?"

"Because you've got the good side. If I move it, your side will become my side. But if my hunch is right, you'll find lots of clams, too."

"Okay."

"If it doesn't work, I'll give you what I dig up. Fair enough?"

Dan pulled the anchor and tossed it four feet to the right. He held the chain carefully, keeping it taut as he let it out.

After the *Morrison Hotel* had drifted all the way back on the anchor, we went to work. My first pull netted twenty-six littleneck clams. It sounded like Dan hauled an entire peck on his pull. We threw down our tongs, and the same thing happened. Dan let out a string of happy curses.

"This is it!" he said. "The mother lode!"

I let out a whoop.

"Don't!" Dan growled, shaking his head. "You start jumping around and celebrating, you'll draw a hundred clammers to this spot. You want that?"

I felt foolish. "No."

"In this business it never pays to advertise your good fortune," Dan said. "We'll work steady. When you've got a good-sized pile, put it in a sack and drag it into the cabin."

"Unculled?"

"Hell, yes. We can do that later." He retied the scarf on his head. "You ready for lunch?"

"But—"

"Don't worry. Those clams aren't going anywhere."

We kept our lunch break short; I couldn't wait to get back to work. Dan threw in two smaller anchors to keep us floating over that exact spot. I pulled up twenty-one clams on my first pull after lunch. I moved eight inches down the boat and threw my tongs back into the water. The clams kept coming. Twenty, fifteen, nineteen, twenty-nine!

"They're thick as bees down there!" Dan murmured.

When Bert landed on the deck he just stood there, bewildered by all the riches we had dredged up. We continued digging. An hour later it had slowed down a bit. Now I was getting *only* eight, nine clams at a time.

"This is a terrible spot," I said. "Awful."

"Wanna move?" Dan asked.

"Oh, yeah, definitely."

"Okay." He went to the front of the boat.

"I'm kidding," I said.

"I'm not." He pulled up the anchor and threw it a few feet to the right. And it worked! Fourteen clams, eighteen, thirty-one!

"How often does this happen—you hit a spot like this?" I asked.

"Twice a year, if that," Dan said.

"I guess we got lucky, huh?"

Dan shook his head. "In my book, you make your own luck."

It was clamming heaven. By two thirty I had hauled four unculled sacks filled with clams into the cabin. Dan had nine! I staggered over and took a long drink of water. My arms were about to fall off.

"There's still more clams down there," he said. "Lots more."

"I can't." I had nothing left. But I was happy.

"Okay, let's go in. We'll pull anchor and cull these clams a half mile from here."

"But what about this spot?" I said.

"What about it?"

"How will we ever . . . find it again?" I asked. "Couldn't we put down a small buoy or something?"

"We got a great gift today. But it's over, kid." He spoke in the softest voice I'd ever heard him use. "Sometimes you've just got to let it go."

I pulled anchor while Dan started the engine. As we moved away I looked back, somehow trying to fix the spot in my memory, but within a few seconds it was just another place on the Great South Bay, indistinguishable from all the water that stretched for miles around us.

It took us forty-five minutes to cull all our clams. Dan finished with seven and a quarter bushels. I dug just under three bushels, my best day by far. When I finished bagging my clams, Dan gave me a standing ovation, and I felt so exhausted and giddy that I spread my dirty arms as wide as I could and did a one-and-a-half flip off the boat into the water.

At the dock I could feel every clammer and wholesaler staring in awe at the enormous mound of clam sacks piled on our boat. If Jazzy had been there, that triumphant moment would have been almost perfect. But when I helped Dan carry all those bushels from the boat to the dock, it still felt good enough for me.

August 14

in THE COVE

"HOW IS OUR FAVORITE BIVALVE EXTRACTOR?" Mom said when I got home. She and Jazzy were sitting at the table, looking at an ad for *Grease,* a Broadway musical they both wanted to see.

"How'd you do today?" Mom asked.

"I made a hundred and ten dollars." I tried to sound nonchalant, but I couldn't keep the grin off my face. They stared at me.

"Really?" Mom asked.

"It was pretty insane. We hit an unbelievable spot. Clams were practically jumping into the boat."

"A hundred and ten dollars in one day?" Jazzy's eyes were huge. "You're rich, boy."

Looking at her, I remembered what it was like a couple of weeks ago, when I really was rich.

"Congratulations, we'll have to celebrate," Mom told me. "I made mussels marinara over linguini."

When we sat down to eat, I helped myself to a big serving. Mom smiled. These days she got a big kick out of my appetite.

"You're going out on Tommy's boat tonight?" Mom asked Jazzy.

Jazzy nodded.

"I know you're a good swimmer, but be careful." Mom looked at me. "How about you? Any plans for the evening?"

"Nope." I went to the sink and rinsed off my plate.

"Aren't you going to have some salad?" Mom asked.

"No, thanks." Hearing about Jazzy and Tommy's date had killed the rest of my appetite.

That night I lay in bed. Jazzy hadn't come home yet, so I felt wired and agitated as usual, and sick of the feeling. I remembered what Dan said that afternoon: *Sometimes you've just got to let it go.* I knew he was right; I had to let Jazzy go. But how?

I had managed to fall asleep when a sound woke me.

"*Pssst!*"

I jumped out of bed and went to the window.

"Who's there?" I whispered.

"It's me, Trevor!"

"What are—"

"Open the window, we gotta talk!"

"The screen doesn't open," I told him. "Go around to the front."

When I opened the front door, Trevor yanked me outside.

"Your cousin's in trouble!" he whispered loudly. "She's in the cove. I ran into Bird Shirsty at the mall, and he told me Tommy's digging there tonight."

I stood there, trying to think, remembering Dan's description of the Conservation boats: big engines, big guns, bad-ass attitude. The last thing I wanted was to barge in on a cozy scene between Jazzy and Tommy, but I couldn't see any way around it.

"Wait here," I told him.

Inside, I picked up the phone and dialed Dan's phone number. I let it ring eight, ten times. Nothing.

"Dan's not home," I said, "but I've got an idea where he might be."

Codfish Bob's was located just a few blocks past the fishing docks. It was a fishermen's bar, watering hole, dive, whatever you want to call it. I asked Trevor to wait outside. The place was loud and smoky. It wasn't hard to pick Dan out at the bar.

"Dan!" I said.

He turned around to eyeball me. I bet I was the last person he expected to see in that place.

"We don't serve minors," the bartender told me. "Not even soda."

"He's mine," Dan said and laughed.

I explained the situation as fast as I could.

"I've got to get Jazzy out of the cove before she gets herself arrested," I said. "I was wondering if maybe I could borrow your boat. I promise—"

"The *Morrison Hotel*? Are you kidding?"

"I swear I'll—"

"No way," Dan cut me off again and shook his head. "Hey, I'm sorry about your cousin, I really am. But she's a big girl. She made her bed—now she can sleep in it. That's how people learn."

I turned around and went outside. Trevor looked up when I came down the stairs. I shook my head and swung up onto my bike.

"What now?" he asked.

"I don't know."

"My brother's got a small boat, like a dinghy, but it's pretty worthless. Doesn't even have an engine."

"Matt."

I turned around to see Dan standing at the top of the stairs. He was looking into the night sky.

"This is the best time to go coving," he said slowly. It almost sounded like he was talking to himself. "No moon, no stars. Night like this, hell, you convince yourself you really are invisible. Most guys wait 'til two, three in the morning. But some guys don't have the patience to wait that long."

He gave me an accusatory look, like I was the one clamming in the cove. Holding the handrail, he walked slowly down the stairs until he was standing in front of me. "If you're going to borrow my boat, you're going to need someone who knows how to navigate at night."

I gave Trevor a quick look. Then we started walking, the three of us, over to the docks. When we stepped onto the *Morrison Hotel*, Dan quickly started the engine. Trevor took a seat in the cabin.

"You better drive," Dan told me. "Ease it back slow."

Putting it into reverse, I twisted the grip on the throttle just a little, the way I'd seen him do all summer.

"Keep way right," Dan said, pointing at the canal. "Water's deep all the way to the bulkhead, so you've got plenty of room."

"Looks pretty calm," Trevor said.

"You can't tell anything until we reach the open bay," Dan told him. "You guys got a plan?"

"Tommy's got a Chris Craft XK 19 with a 210-horsepower inboard engine," I pointed out. "That boat is fast. He's going to hear our engine. There's no way we'll catch him if he runs."

"I've got an idea," Trevor offered. "We've got to surprise them. I say we make a wide circle and come in from the south. Then we turn off the engine and let the wind blow us in."

"Drift into the cove?" Dan looked over at me and smiled. "Now there's a crazy-ass plan if I've ever heard one. But it just might work."

When we reached the bay, I pushed the throttle and headed southeast. It felt weird driving when I couldn't see a thing, but Dan seemed to know where we were going. A half hour later he signaled me to cut the engine. The wind caught us and began to push us along. The swell was bigger than it looked, and it turned the *Morrison Hotel* sideways, rocking us back and forth. Dan crawled below and returned with a tiny engine.

"How do you like this eggbeater?" Dan asked. He actually seemed to be enjoying the adventure. He attached the engine to the stern. "This works off the battery, so it don't have much power, but at least it'll keep us heading straight. And it's dead quiet."

When Dan started the engine it barely made a whisper. We kept moving toward the cove. There was no moon, so the darkness felt thick. Six, eight minutes passed. Suddenly we heard the clink of metal on metal. Dan moved his finger over his lips. He switched off the tiny engine, made his finger into a gun, and pointed.

"Bingo," he said softly. "They're dead ahead. When we get closer, you start the big engine and make a run at him. He's still got to pull anchor. We'll try to board him before he has a chance to get going."

We drifted closer. Now I could make out the outlines of the Chris Craft, less than a hundred yards ahead.

"Get ready," Dan whispered to me. "It will already be in gear when you start it."

I grabbed the starter cord and gave a fierce tug. We shot forward, engine roaring, streaking toward them. Dan turned on a powerful light that illuminated the boat before us. The Chris Craft rode low in the water, and it had a sleek windshield but no cabin. I spotted Tommy, shirtless, frantically pulling up his tongs. Jazzy stood beside him, looking frightened. I realized they both probably figured we were Conservation boats trying to nail them. Tommy yelled something to Jazzy. She went to the front of the boat and started pulling the anchor.

"Cut the line!" Tommy screamed. But it was too late—we were on top of them. I threw the engine into reverse and maneuvered us next to the Chris Craft. I jumped onto

Tommy's boat and tied off our line with one quick knot. I heard our engine stop just as Tommy fired up his inboard. I was right by Jazzy, close enough to touch her.

"Come on," I told her.

She looked at me in disbelief. Tommy knifed between us and swung at me. I ducked—the punch grazed the top of my head. Trevor barreled past me and tackled Tommy. When Tommy went down, I found the key in the ignition and shut off his engine.

"What are you doing?" Jazzy screamed at Trevor. "Get off him!"

Tommy got up, swearing, and twisted out of Trevor's grip. He squinted into Dan's powerful light.

"What's your problem?" Tommy bellowed.

"You're breaking the law!" Then Dan pointed at Jazzy. "And if you're with him, you're breaking it, too."

"The law!" Tommy laughed.

"I'm willing to radio the Conservation folks," Dan said, "if that would hurry things along."

"I'm not going!" Jazzy moved closer to Tommy, defiant.

"You want to get arrested?" Dan asked her. "It's a thousand-dollar fine, mandatory, if they catch you clamming here."

Tommy yelled, "It's none of your freakin' business, Grandpa!"

"Oh, really?" Dan grinned as if he'd been expecting that. He jumped from his boat toward Tommy's. He could move fast for a big man, but just as Dan stepped, a swell rose up and pulled the boats apart, causing his right foot to slip off the side of the Garvey. He fell, hitting his head hard on the edge of the Chris Craft before he fell into the dark water.

Tommy actually laughed.

"Dan!" I screamed. I jumped back to the *Morrison Hotel* and held my breath, staring down at the water. A long moment passed before Dan's furious face popped up to the surface again. He was bleeding from a spot a few inches above his ear.

"Here!" I yelled, throwing him a line. The *Morrison Hotel* had a flat, low deck, which helped when you had to climb from the water. Dan muscled himself onto the boat and stood glaring at Tommy O'Rourke.

"Are you okay?" I asked.

"I'm a hell of a lot better than the other guy you fished out of the bay," Dan told me. He wiped his face and pointed at Jazzy. "Get onto this boat, sweetheart, before things get ugly."

Her face was set, lips pressed together, as she stepped onto the *Morrison Hotel*. Trevor and I followed.

"Dump your clams," Dan told Tommy. "Now."

Tommy swore softly and emptied both sacks back into the bay. Dan waited until Tommy pulled anchor, started his engine, and gunned it. Tommy's boat disappeared into the night. I went into the cabin and pulled out the first-aid kit, but Dan brushed me away, his wet shirt clinging to his back. He signaled me to start the engine. Then he turned on the Doors and we began moving through the dark waters of the cove.

UΠFiΠiSHED BUSIΠESS

THE NEXT DAY Dan and I stopped at the coffee stand before we got on the boat. It was almost nine o'clock—much later than we usually started work. Darlene motioned at the bandage on Dan's head. "What happened?"

"Shark bit me," Dan said, deadpan. "Are those blueberry muffins?"

Darlene gave Dan a skeptical look. "Yep. Made them myself."

Dan bought two muffins and walked over to the *Morrison Hotel*. Darlene looked at my face closely.

"Your nose is a little sunburned." She walked around the counter and put a dab of sunscreen on it.

"I think it's too late for that." I stood there, trying to keep still.

"It's never too late," Darlene said, holding my eyes with hers.

I figured that was my cue. "You want to go to the movies sometime? *The Exorcist* is supposed to be good. Unless you don't like scary movies."

"I love horror!" She smiled. "Turn around."

Darlene took out a piece of paper, put it against my back, and wrote her phone number on it.

Dan and I were both tired from the night before, so we took it slow. Rain started falling just as we sat down for our lunch break. While we ate, the rain got harder, and it started washing away the muck we'd dredged up.

"Want to go in the cabin?" Dan asked, rubbing the side of his head. His cut hadn't needed stitches, but the bandage was itchy.

"I'm okay." The morning had been muggy, and the rain felt refreshing.

"Your cousin still mad at you?" Dan asked.

"I imagine so. I didn't see her this morning."

"She'll get over it. She probably doesn't realize it, but you did her a big favor by getting her out of there."

"You did me a big favor, too," I said. "I appreciate having this job."

He nodded. "You got enough money to buy the Boston Whaler?"

"Just about."

"Guess I won't be seeing you much after that." Dan held out a piece of crust for Bert. The seagull darted in, neatly grabbed it, and scooted away. Sitting there, eating my lunch, surrounded by all the clams, crabs, seaweed, sea worms, scungilli, wild sponges, and stinking mud, it hit me: *I'm really going to miss all this.*

The house was empty when I got home. I cleaned up and biked back to the fishing docks. There was a line of customers, baymen and fishermen, waiting at Darlene's stand, and I was tempted to stop and chat with her, but I didn't. I was on a mission. I approached Frank's truck.

"Hey, Matt. What's up?"

I swallowed. "I'm here to get my pay."

He glanced around, confused. "I already paid you for today."

"I know," I replied. "I'm here to get the money you owe me."

He stopped smiling. "I don't owe you any money, son. I pay my clammers every day. Cash on the barrel. You know that."

"Look." I opened up my notebook to show him. "I've been keeping a log all summer—the date, how much the clams weighed on your scale. Here, I put how much I should have been paid. Here's what you paid me. And here's the difference."

"Prices have been going down," Frank said coolly.

"That's not the point." My heart was hammering, but I had no choice except to keep talking. "Here, two weeks ago, I dug fifty-two pounds, and you were paying seventy-five cents a pound. That comes out to thirty-nine dollars. But you paid me only thirty-seven. That kind of thing happened fifteen times this summer. It comes out to eighty-six dollars."

His face got hard. "Are you saying I cheated you, Matt?"

I was ready for him to say that.

"You underpaid me eighty-six dollars," I said carefully. My mouth felt like a desert. I pointed at the number at the bottom of the page. "You can add it up yourself."

Frank DiFeo stared at me. "You've got no proof."

"I've got this," I said, holding up the notebook.

"Son, I don't know what the hell you're talking about." He shook his head and turned to watch a tall man unloading sacks of clams from his Garvey. "You made up those numbers, far as I can tell. I'm done doing business with you. Understand? From now on you can peddle your clams somewhere else, if you can find anybody who'll buy them."

He turned away. I didn't particularly like the tone he used to talk to me, the way you'd speak to a little kid. I stood for a second, but there was nothing more I could say, so I got on my bike and rode away.

I didn't mention this incident to Dan while we were clamming the next day. I figured it wasn't his problem. We found Frank DiFeo standing by his truck, as usual, when we came in to sell our clams. I carried my sack of clams to the truck parked beside Frank's. A man sat there, legs dangling down from the opening in back.

"My name is Matt Carter," I said. "Are you buying clams?"

The man glanced over at Frank DiFeo. At the docks there's an unspoken rule that clammers always stick with the same wholesaler.

"Do you have a clam license?" the man asked.

"Yes." I pulled it out to show him.

The man squinted at it. Then he reached into my sack of clams, took out a handful, and examined them. "These look pretty clean."

"They're clean, all right."

"My name's Carl. Carl Wilson." He shook my hand and hoisted my clams onto his scale. "I'm paying twenty-nine dollars a bushel. Let's see what you got."

Dan had been too busy unloading his clams to notice that I'd gone to a different truck. He walked over to me.

"What are you doing?" He seemed amused.

"Yesterday I talked to Frank and told him he owed me money from underpaying me all summer. I showed him my notebook. Comes to eighty-six bucks. He told me I was full of it and he wasn't going to buy from me anymore, and I don't want to sell to him, either."

Dan turned to Frank.

"Here you go, Dan, two hundred forty-five pounds." Frank held out a wad of money. "Comes to a hundred and fifty-five."

Dan ignored the money. "Matt says you've been shorting him."

"Aw, come on. I've been buying clams here for five years. I pay honest weight, fair and square. Kid's got an overactive imagination."

"I don't think so," Dan said evenly. "I've worked with this kid all summer. If he says you owe it to him, well, you probably do."

"I don't owe him diddly," Frank insisted. By now several other clammers had stopped to watch.

"Well, then, I guess you don't owe me diddly, either." Dan grabbed a bushel of his clams and started to leave.

"Hold it, hold it," Frank said. He swore loudly and shook his head. Maybe he wasn't completely honest, but he wasn't stupid. He opened his cash box, counted out eighty-six dollars, and slapped the bills into my hand.

"Thanks," I said. He swore again as he walked away.

POLTERGEISTS AND PACHYDERMS

GETTING THE MONEY that Frank DiFeo owed me felt like an actual happy ending, which doesn't happen very often, except on TV. But with Jazzy and me I didn't have much hope for the same. We were in different worlds, and her visit was nearly over. In eleven days she'd be making the long flight back to Hawaii.

Jazzy once said that jazz music can take a sharp turn and change without warning. That's what improvisation is all about. But after everything that had happened between us, I had no idea how to change the music. So I simply avoided her. It was like the end of a football or basketball game where you had gotten your butt kicked and you just wanted the game to be over. That's what I was doing with Jazzy. I was running out the clock.

At supper, Jazzy didn't say anything about what had happened in the cove, so I didn't mention it, either. After we cleaned up, she brought her guitar into the den. She said she had written a new song. I had zero appetite for a Tommy song, so I tried to slip past the den doorway and duck into my bedroom.

But Mom spotted me. "Aren't you going to come listen?"

With my escape route cut off, I had no choice but to join them.

"Sure."

I stood, leaning against the side of the couch. Jazzy took a minute to get the guitar tuned. The song began with an instrumental part, haunting and slow, before she started to sing.

> *There's a beach in Waimanalo*
> *just the sea and breezy air.*
> *Mostly locals know about it,*
> *but I can take you there.*
>
> *Kaiona Beach, that's where I wanna go,*
> *you can sleep on the sand when the sun sinks low;*
> *Kaiona Beach, that's where I wanna go,*
> *I'll whisper to you when I pull you close.*

The song, and the way she sang it, had a soulful feeling. When it ended, Mom and I stayed quiet. Clapping didn't seem like the right response to a song like that.

"That one sounded a little sad," Mom said gently. "You've been away from home a long time. Are you feeling homesick?"

"Not really." When she looked around the room, her eyes brushed mine. "I don't know why I'm feeling blue."

The following day we planned to go out for a lobster dinner, Jazzy's treat. Lobster happens to be my all-time favorite food; still, I wanted to avoid an awkward restaurant scene, with Jazzy and me sitting there pretending to be friendly. I needed to come up with an excuse—airtight and waterproof—that Mom would find believable. I figured that shouldn't be too hard.

Jazzy was sitting at the table when I walked into the kitchen. I was filthy, as usual. Her guitar leaned on the chair next to her. I saw that she was working on the crossword.

"Ho, Matt." She offered a small smile.

I mumbled a hello. "Where's Mom?"

"She called and said she might be late. What's the capital of Oregon? Begins with S."

"Salem." I had memorized the state capitals in fourth grade; I still knew most of them.

"Yeah, that works." She wrote it down.

"I'm going to clean up," I said, edging away.

"Wait." From her chair she gazed up, eyes wide, almost pleading. "Help me with one more: '1950s circular fad.' Starts with *h*."

I gave her a blank look.

"'Hula hoop'!" she cried, answering her own question. Her whole face lit up. "I used to have one—I was really good at it!"

"I bet." I peered over her shoulder, scanning the clues. "Did you get 23 across? 'Golden swimmer.' That's got to be Mark Spitz."

"Spitz!" She looked at me, impressed. "You want to help?"

"Shouldn't we wait for Mom?"

"I asked when she called. She said to go ahead without her."

Jazzy moved her guitar away from the chair beside her. Hesitating a moment, hoping I didn't smell too terrible, I pulled out the chair and sat down. She slid the puzzle between us.

"How about 13 down?" she asked. "'Hairpiece,' three letters."

"'Rug'?"

She laughed.

"'Ghosts,' twelve letters." I shook my head. "That's a rough one."

"'Poltergeists'?"

"Does it fit?" I asked.

"I think so . . . yeah, it does."

Sometimes when you're doing a crossword you fall into a rhythm and you suddenly find yourself solving the clues one after the other, no problem, bang-bang-bang-bang. During that time you feel like a genius. That's what happened now: Jazzy and I caught on fire.

She read, "'Rush the passer.'"

"'Blitz.'" I waited for her to jot that down. "'Theatrical works.'"

"'Plays,'" she said.

I shook my head. "Nope, doesn't fit. *Six* letters. Starts with a *D*."

"'Dramas.' Hah!"

After that, there was no stopping us. Uriah: Heep. Killer whale: Orca. Get a ___ of this: Load. End: Terminate. Boo-boo: Error. Scout's reward: Badge. Bend: Warp. L.A. hoopsters: Lakers. Rock-concert utopia: Woodstock. One by one we knocked them down. Maybe the puzzle was unusually easy—who cared? Soon there were only two unsolved clues left.

She said: "40 across, 'Express regret.'"

"That's easy." I looked at her. "'Apologize.' If it fits."

"It fits. You know I already did, Matt." She was speaking very softly. "Apologize, I mean."

"I know." I wasn't sure what else to say, so I read the last clue, "50 down. 'Pachyderm.'"

"Elephants are pachyderms, aren't they?" she asked.

Seeing that the word fit, Jazzy let out a triumphant squeal. I smiled. We almost hugged each other, but didn't.

"I love elephants!" she cried.

"They say that elephants never forget," I pointed out.

Her dark eyes turned solemn. "Do they ever . . . forgive?"

"I think so." I nodded.

Jazzy offered her hand. "Truce?"

"Okay." We shook hands formally, like a couple of grown-ups.

"I like it better this way," she said softly.

I nodded. "Hey, I liked that new song."

"Thanks."

Casually, I said, "Did you play that one for Tommy? I know . . . it's none of my business."

"No!" Jazzy made a face. "We broke up."

At that very moment Mom burst into the kitchen.

"Aunt Alice!" Jazzy exclaimed. "We did it—we finished the crossword!"

"Congratulations!" She came over to look. "Very nice. Hey, I'm starving! Is anybody else hungry? I heard a rumor that we're going out for dinner."

"For lobster," Jazzy corrected her. "And I'm paying."

Mom's face had a pained expression. "But lobster is so expensive! We'd be just as happy with pasta, or pizza."

"Do you have any idea how much you pay for Maine lobster in Hawaii?" Jazzy asked. "Probably three times what it costs here! Anyway, Mom gave me money to take you out to dinner at least once. She'll kill me if I don't spend it."

She looked at me expectantly. I hadn't planned on going, but the thought of warm, buttery lobster had my mouth watering.

"I'll need to clean up."

"Hurry up," Mom told me.

In the shower I turned the hot water on full-blast. *We broke up.* Amazing how three tiny words like that could send my spirits soaring.

You make your own luck, Dan once said. I wondered if that was true. Was it better if luck was earned or if it just fell from the sky? I honestly didn't know, but it seemed like, finally, my luck had taken a turn for the better.

TALKING STORY

JAZZY WANTED to come clamming. Dan agreed. He turned on the Doors, loud, as we headed down the canal toward the Great South Bay. By now I knew the lyrics to every song: "Roadhouse Blues," "Waiting for the Sun," "You Make Me Real," "Peace Frog," "Blue Sunday," "Ship of Fools." Those songs had been the soundtrack for my feelings about Jazzy, so it felt strange to hear them with her actually on the boat.

In the middle of "Land Ho!" Dan cut the engine and shut off the music. I loved that first moment of quiet, just after the engine stopped and before we started clamming. I threw in the anchor; Dan lifted down the tongs. I made my first pull while Dan tied his red scarf over his head.

Jazzy was amazed at all the little creatures we pulled up. For a while she kept herself busy pushing small crabs back into the water. When we took our morning break, Jazzy passed around some chocolate chip cookies she had baked herself.

"They're a little burnt," she said sheepishly.

Dan smiled. "We aren't fussy."

"That's for sure," I agreed. The cookies tasted great.

"What do you think of the *Morrison Hotel*?" Dan asked. "This isn't your first ride on it."

There was an awkward silence. Jazzy just looked at him.

"The things we do for love," Dan said.

"Love!" Jazzy rolled her eyes. "Anyway, I'm sorry you got hurt that night."

Dan laughed. "Are you kidding? I'm a Vietnam vet. It takes more than a little knock on the head to dent this skull."

We broke for lunch at noon. Jazzy was delighted when Bert landed on the shade side of the boat. She gathered a dozen broken clams for him. "There you go, cutie!"

"Bert is spoiled rotten, but he's good company," Dan said. "Even for a solitary guy like me, it can get lonely out here. I'm going to miss working with your cousin. Which reminds me, Matt. I've got something for you."

He went over to the tongs I'd been using all summer and lay them down next to me. "These are yours now."

"Thanks." That meant a lot. "I'd like to keep clamming with you. I mean, if that's okay."

Dan peered at me. "You haven't bought the Boston Whaler?"

"Not yet." I still needed to save about a hundred dollars more.

Dan retied the scarf on his head. "Your clam license is good for a whole year. You know when I leave the dock in the morning. You've got your own set of tongs and your side of this boat whenever you want it."

"Thanks, Dan."

We went back to work. All day the bay water had been like polished glass. Jazzy came and stood beside me.

"What's that, Matt?" She pointed at some rough waters near Fire Island. I told her about the One O'Clock Chop. I explained how it would work its way to us and make us swing around on our anchor until we were facing south. You could see that breeze moving toward us. It was like a force of nature.

In eight days she would be gone.

Next morning Mom and Jazzy would be heading into Manhattan. They had a list of things they wanted to do—tons of shopping and sightseeing—plus Mom had bought tickets for *Grease*. She had gone to bed early to get ready for the big day. But Jazzy said she didn't feel tired, and I didn't, either.

We went out to the porch. Jazzy played a few songs, including the one I was once certain she wrote about me, not that I'd ever ask.

> *He's my kine boy . . .*
> *got my kine smile . . .*
> *and my kine kiss . . .*
> *he's my kine boy . . .*

"What's that last chord?" I asked when she finished playing.

"D." She offered me her guitar. "You want me to show you a few chords? It's not hard."

I shook my head. "Clam tongs, that's the only instrument I know how to play. It makes money instead of music."

Jazzy laughed and strummed her guitar. The summer air was warm and very still. For some reason it made me feel restless.

"Let's go find a place where we can talk story," she said.

I gave her a funny look. "Talk story?"

"That's how we say *chitchat* in Hawaii. Talk story means shoot the breeze. Can we go take a walk or something?"

"Okay."

Jazzy followed me down the porch steps. By some silent understanding we went through the back yard to the path that led into the woods. We walked side by side, Hansel and Gretel stumbling through the forest, trying to find our way home, even though the crumbs we'd left were long gone. A few minutes later we reached our old hideaway.

"I never photographed this spot, but I wanted to come back here one more time so I'd fix it in my mind. It's really peaceful here. And it's ours."

Was ours, I thought. The place felt different now. *We* felt different. The words we spoke seemed to be Bubble Wrapped, surrounded by pauses and silences to cushion them from breaking against each other.

"You really should come to Hawaii," Jazzy said. "We've got plenty of room. Aunt Alice could come, too."

"Just like that?" I asked.

"Sure, why not? I know the most amazing swimming hole, a place that's not on any tourist map. The water's crystal clear. There's a waterfall and you can climb behind it. It has a rock ledge about ten inches wide where you can sit and let the water tickle the front of your nose. You've *got* to see it, Matt!"

"Flying to Hawaii is pretty expensive," I pointed out.

"They have special fares a couple of times a year. If you fly out to Montana to see your father, you're already halfway to Hawaii. When are you going to go see him next?"

"I'm not sure." I looked away from her.

"What's wrong?" she asked.

"I don't know. I'm kind of pissed off at him. For a bunch of reasons."

"Yeah? Does he know why you're mad?"

"I doubt it. I can't really talk to him like I can talk to Mom. Or Dan. I never could."

"I'll *never* talk to my father again." She sounded sad. "But you can still talk to yours. Think about it, Matt. You've got to keep trying."

"It's pretty hopeless."

"No, it's not," she insisted. "Things can change. Look at us. We barely spoke for two weeks. Now we're talking again like friends."

Kneeling down at the spring, I took a long drink. The icy water made my head throb.

"You're going to buy your boat this week, aren't you?"

I nodded. "Wednesday."

"I won't get to see it," she said sadly.

"Don't worry, I'll send you a picture," I told her.

"Will you miss me?" Jazzy asked softly.

"Yeah," I admitted. But I could feel myself holding back, big-time. After all the heartache I'd gone through, I didn't want to feel it again. I couldn't take any more bleeding.

She flipped off her sandals, stuck one foot into the water, and gasped. She kept her foot in the water as long as she could. Then she stepped out and spent a few seconds rubbing warmth back into her foot.

"A girl could get hypothermia around here." She started to move to the salt lick, but I stopped her.

"Don't." I didn't want it to be the same as before. It couldn't be.

Jazzy moved in front of me. Her hands found my shoulders. I was glad to be with her again. But something seemed wrong. There was a question I needed to ask her, one that would bother me forever if I didn't get some kind of answer. The thing is, I didn't exactly know how to put it into words.

Her hands moved up to my neck, but I twisted away from her.

"What's wrong?"

I didn't answer.

"Matt?"

"What happened?" I finally said.

"Huh?"

"What happened," I repeated, "at the yacht club that night?"

"Oh," she said, finally understanding. "Tommy."

I had that punched-in-the-gut feeling that made it hard to draw a complete breath. Both my hands had formed themselves into tense fists. Picturing Tommy on his spiffy little red boat, it occurred to me that one of these days I would really have to kick the crap out of him.

"I'm sorry I hurt you—" she began.

"You already said that!" I was kicking myself for even bringing up the subject. I hated this conversation, but there was no turning back now.

"Then what?" she asked.

"I still don't get it. One day you and I are . . . close, right? And then, *boom*, it's over."

Jazzy crouched down to the spring. For a long moment she stayed quiet.

"You're right. We were close." She spoke in a half whisper. "Maybe I was scared we were getting *too* close. You know? I mean, we're cousins."

"So that was it? The main reason you broke it off?"

"Part of it."

"And the other part?"

She drew herself up until she was standing before me. "I like you, Matt," she said hesitantly. "A lot. But I liked Tommy, too. That night at the yacht club you weren't there . . . and Tommy asked me to dance. At first I said no, but then I realized I did want to dance with him. He asked me again, and that time I said yes. Things just sort of went from there."

I could picture the whole scene—the loud music, Tommy giving her the eye, the two of them flirting with each other. It hurt, what she said, but not as much as I expected.

"Well, thanks for being honest," I finally said. "At least you didn't make up some lame story."

She took a step closer. It was too dark to see the solemn, soulful look on her face, but I didn't need to see it. By now I had memorized every detail of her face—her lips, her dark eyes, the waterfall of black hair—right down to a faint trace of acne on one side of her chin.

"Anyway," she said, "that was then, but now is now."

Oddly enough, I understood what she meant by that. We hugged. Then I kissed her, and she kissed back, humming, leaning into me.

A PACKET OF SALT

WE DROVE TO LaGuardia Airport. Jazzy wore black pants, a daisy-print blouse Mom had bought her as a present, sandals, and her puka-shell necklace.

"You have an hour-and-fifteen-minute stopover in LA before you get the flight to Honolulu," Mom said when we reached the departure gate. "That's not bad."

Jazzy's lower lip started to tremble. She and Mom cried, hugging each other, saying soft things that I couldn't hear.

Jazzy wiped her eyes. Then she turned to me.

"Bye, Matt." She gave me a fierce hug. I had an insane urge to kiss her one last time, but with Mom standing there, all I could do was brush Jazzy's cheek with my lips.

"Hey, I almost forgot." From a brown paper bag I pulled out a flower lei made out of honeysuckle blossoms. I thought it was kind of amateurish when I made it, though it looked pretty when I put it around her neck.

"You made this?" Jazzy asked in amazement.

I smiled.

"It's beautiful!" She started to cry again when I hugged her a second time. She looked up, and I had a worried thought: when would I see her again?

"They're calling your flight," Mom said gently.

"Okay, I'd better go." Jazzy bit her lip. "Thank you so much for everything. Bye!"

She walked away with sunlight behind her. For a few seconds all I could see was Jazzy's silhouette, waving. Then she handed her ticket to the agent and disappeared through the gate.

Mom and I drove home from the airport. For some reason I felt exhausted.

"A honeysuckle lei." Mom turned to look at me. "How did you think of that?"

"I don't know." I shrugged. "She likes honeysuckle."

"Very sweet." She sighed. "I'm sure going to miss that girl."

"I know," I replied, swallowing. "Hey, Mom, think we could maybe go visit her?"

I always could count on Mom to be predictable. *A trip to Hawaii would be awfully expensive*—that's what she would say. And how could I argue with that? But this time Mom threw me a curve. She winked at me.

"I'm already working on it."

Mom dropped me at home and then went food shopping. With Jazzy gone, the house seemed way too quiet. I went to my bedroom. On my pillow I found one of those little packets of salt that you get at restaurants. Jazzy must have put it there. Lying on my bed, I stared at the packet.

I felt empty. I still had a week before school started up again, but the best part of summer was over. What did I have to look forward to now?

The phone rang, making me jump. I expected it to be Trevor, or maybe Dad, so I was surprised when I heard a girl's voice.

"Hello?"

I got excited. "Jazzy?"

"No, it's Darlene."

"Oh, yeah, hi, Darlene."

There was a long pause. "Who's Jazzy?"

"Well, she's my cousin." I swore at myself—what was wrong with me? "She spent the summer with us. She's flying home today—to Hawaii. I just came home from the airport."

"Oh."

"What's up?" I finally said.

"My uncle's having a big end-of-the-summer beach party at his house," she said. "On Saturday. He lives in Kismet, on Fire Island. Do you want to come?"

"A beach party? Yeah, sure."

"Well, good."

A thought crossed my mind: maybe, just possibly, I could take Darlene to the party in my Boston Whaler. Tomorrow afternoon I would go to Hunt's Marina and buy the boat for nine hundred and fifty dollars. I planned to pay for it with cash. In my head I pictured Darlene and me flying across the Great South Bay toward Jones Beach.

"It's going to be a blast," Darlene was saying. "My uncle's in a rock band, so there should be great music. He told me it'll be a combination barbecue and clambake. Do you like clams?"

"Clams?" I laughed. "Well, yeah, as a matter of fact I do."